The Privilege of The Sex and other stories

Other books by Pat Bryan

What Else You Got?—40 Years of Mis-Spent Youth In The Ad Game
Farnol: The Man Who Wrote Best-Sellers

The Privilege of The Sex and other stories

Stories, articles and poems previously unpublished, or uncollected in book form, from one of the world's best-selling authors.

Jeffery Farnol
(compiled and edited by Pat Bryan)

Writers Club Press
San Jose New York Lincoln Shanghai

The Privilege of The Sex and other stories

All Rights Reserved © 2002 by Jane Farnol Curtis and Pat Bryan

No part of this book may be reproduced or transmitted in any form or by any means, graphic, electronic, or mechanical, including photocopying, recording, taping, or by any information storage retrieval system, without the permission in writing from the publisher.

Writers Club Press
an imprint of iUniverse, Inc.

For information address:
iUniverse, Inc.
5220 S. 16th St., Suite 200
Lincoln, NE 68512
www.iuniverse.com

Several of these stories, articles and poems have appeared in various publications over the past century, and acknowledgement is made, where appropriate, in the Contents page and in the introduction to each.

ISBN: 0-595-23421-6

Printed in the United States of America

To my father, Harold Bryan, who first introduced me to the works of Jeffery Farnol, this book is dedicated.

Contents

How I Began 1
    T.P.'s Weekly, February 14, 1913
Boots 6
    Unpublished
The Oubliette..9
    Young's Magazine, March 15, 1912
New Romney Camp 22
    Daily Telegraph, September 5, 1921
A Tale of My Grandfather 31
    BBC Light Programme, August 6, 1951
Dempsey/Carpentier Fight 37
    Daily Mail, June 25—July 4, 1921
Rejecting Philomela 59
    Good Housekeeping, March 1912
These Million-Dollar Fights 73
    London Evening Standard, July 26, 1928
Hove..77
    Foreword to promotional booklet, 1933
To My Spouse—Our Pilk 86
    Unpublished
Merry England In Brave New Days 88
    Sunday Empire News, December 24, 1944
Fear 93
    Unpublished
Old London Town 95
    Unpublished
The Roller 97
    Daily Mail, October 7, 1944

A Letter To Jane 104
    Unpublished
Our Giant 107
    Unknown
The Privilege of The Sex 109
    Unpublished

List of Illustrations

Cover illustration from a drawing by Edmund Blampied, originally published in 'The Chronicles of The Imp" by Sampson Low, Marston & Co., Ltd in 1915.

Foreword

Jeffery Farnol was born in 1878 in Edgbaston, near Birmingham, but moved to Lee in Kent at an early age. He started his writing career there in the late 1890s with the acceptance of one or two short stories. However, it was not until after his marriage to a young woman from the United States, and their move to New York in 1902, that he began to gain some minor acceptance as an author, and it was not until 1910 that he had his first major success. In that year 'The Broad Highway' was published, first in England, and then in the U.S., and became the best selling fiction book in the world in 1911. He, with his family, returned to England, and his popularity continued; he was to publish a book a year, sometimes two, until his death in 1952. This was in addition to many short stories and articles for newspapers and magazines which were never published in book form.

In 2000, when I first conceived the idea of writing a full biography of Farnol, my research led me to sources for many of these stories and articles. With the help of fellow Farnol-lovers in England and the U.S., I was able to collect copies of most of them, and it then occurred to me that, in addition to the biography ('Farnol: The Man Who Wrote Best-Sellers', Writers Club Press, 2001), I might also compile, edit and publish a collection of these 'lost' Farnols.

It proved to be an interesting, exciting, and sometimes frustrating task. I would discover what I believed to be a hidden 'gem', only to find that it had subsequently appeared in book form under another title. A story listed in their files by Farnol's agents as 'Another Way', for example, actually appeared as 'Silent Weapons' in Collier's Magazine in 1931. I obtained a copy of it, only to have my hopes dashed when it turned out to be a serialisation of his book 'Charmian, Lady Vibart.' And this happened on a number of occasions; Farnol, bless his heart, was too canny a craftsman to let a good story go to waste—and who can blame him?

I persevered, however. With kind permission and help from Jane (Farnol) Curtis in Australia, Jeffery's daughter, who also supplied some previously unpublished manuscripts of her father's, the result is this book. For those familiar with Jeffery Farnol's work, this should prove a new treat. For those who are new to Farnol, we hope this may prove a pleasant introduction and an encouragement to read some of his novels, and discover what it is we Farnol fans like about him. His many books can still be found on the shelves of used and rare book stores around the world; some 2500 are listed on the Internet through companies like Amazon.com, bibliofind.com, Barnes and Noble, or abebooks.com.

My thanks are due to Mark Blanchard, Julia Riding, Mike Smith, Bob Ellenwood, and Jane and Brian Curtis, who helped in the search for this material; and to Ian and Doth Edmondson-Noble, who keep all we Farnol fans in touch through their web site.

The good stuff in this book is all from Jeffery Farnol; the rest is mine.

Port Hope, Ontario, Canada
June, 2002

This is perhaps the only autobiographical piece that Jeffery Farnol ever wrote. It appeared in 'T.P.'s Weekly', a popular English literary magazine founded by T.P. O'Connor, on February 14, 1913, after the outstanding success of Farnol's world's best-seller 'The Broad Highway'. It was only one of a spate of articles about Jeffery Farnol that were published in literary journals of the time, in addition to a number of 'newsy' snippets that appeared in publications like 'The Bookman'.

HOW I BEGAN

How I began! Well, it must have been when, as a very little lad, I used to sit, round of eye, listening for hours while my father read aloud to us that the first idea of some day telling stories of my own first possessed me. Through my father's reading, Fenimore Cooper, Scott, Dickens, Thackeray, Dumas, Stevenson—all were familiar to me from my earliest boyhood. I well remember my brother and I, long after we had been sent to bed, sitting in our nightshirts outside the door of the room wherein my father was reading "The Count of Monte Cristo" to my mother, while she was busy with her needle, and our vicinity being betrayed by an inopportune sneeze. This must have happened when I was no more than eight years old, and from that time we were duly admitted, for an extra hour, to the evening readings. I can never be grateful enough to my father for those long, delightful hours when he—an excellent reader, varying his voice as the characters required—made the stories live for us.

Idle Hours and Mischief.

And here I would take leave to say that if were this a more common practice with parents, most surely would a love of literature be encouraged, to reappear in their children in after years in some form or other. If home were made, as it should be, the most attractive place on earth, and the warm sympathy of the home maintained as the boys grew older, those idle hours of lounging and vacant-mindedness wherein the germ of so much evil takes its first inception would be unknown. As a schoolboy of ten or twelve, during any moments we could steal or make out of the time allotted for "prep."—that haunting incubus—or other legitimate schoolwork, I always had an eager audience for the tales—long-drawn out and of wild and wonderful adventure—which I wove out of a perfervid imagination for the benefit of my schoolfellows. I often wonder if those boys—now grave solicitors and men of business, busy doctors, and stern soldiers, doing their man's duty in all parts of the Empire—ever think of the marvellous yarns I used to spin, the moving accidents by field and flood—mostly flood, for I had all a boy's affection for a really blood-thirsty pirate—and, supposing they have read my books, if they find anything in them to remind them of their one-time chum!

Chimney Climber.

After I left school, with a laudable endeavour to wean me from my bookish habits, my father sent me, at the age of seventeen, to a firm of engineers and brassfounders in Birmingham. Here I worked hard at the forge, among other things, and Black George is undoubtedly an outcrop of this time of my life. It is a fact that a great deal of fighting came my way just then, and an intimate knowledge of the rough side of working-class life, which has largely coloured my views of the working-man and his surroundings. I fear the only way in which I distinguished myself at this portion of my career was by climbing for a wager—two shillings, I think, was the amount—to the top of the factory chimney, about a hundred and twenty feet, and hanging my handkerchief, flagwise, from the lightning-conductor to show I'd been there. This escapade, together with my propensity for story-telling and sketching, which followed me to the workshop and the forge, was the end of my career in Birmingham. It was no uncommon thing for the foreman—and, worse still, the principal—to find me in the dinner hour the centre of a gaping crowd of men and boys, who were listening open-mouthed while I regaled them with stories from the classics, vividly touched up, no doubt, or making a rough drawing of some scowling diffident sitter.

Pearls of Wisdom.

A worse offense, from the point of view of those in authority over me, was my habit of always keeping a notebook beside me, in which the various pearls of wisdom that occurred to me were industriously jotted down. This, of course, could not be tolerated, and ended in my coming to blows with that god of the workshop, my foreman; so I was returned on my parents' hands, "no good for work—always writing"! Then ensued a time when I stayed at home and wrote stories, poems—anything and everything. A few short stories got themselves into print—just enough, with the encouragement I got at home, to help me over the thorny first years of effort. I had a natural aptitude for drawing, and during these years studied line and figure drawing under Loudon, at the Westminster School. It was about this time that I became acquainted with a certain shy, quick-eyed fellow-student, who is now the well-known Japanese artist and author, Yoshio Markino.

The "Ancient."

My favourite recreation at this time was cycling. All the high roads and by-roads of Kent, Surrey, and Sussex became familiar to me as, sometimes with a chum or brother, sometimes alone, I wheeled between the flowery hedgerows and quenched my thirst and ate enormous meals at the quaint wayside taverns. I remember it was on one of these week-end excursions, a hot Sunday evening in August found me sitting, with my friend Mr. H.London Pope, in the porch of the "Bull", at Sissinghurst, where we had made our headquarters, resting and washing the dust from our throats with good brown ale, and watching the villagers wending their way to church, that I first saw the "Ancient". There he was, tall hat, smock-frock, shrewd, wrinkled face, and gnarled hands grasping his knobbly staff, just as I have described him in "The Broad Highway". And that was the very first inception of the book, though it was not until several years afterwards that it came to be written—not until I had left home, and the fresh, green, Kentish lanes, and was living in New York, managing to eke out a not too luxurious living by publishing stories in the magazines and by scene-painting at the Astor Theatre.

"The Broad Highway."

So it was in the intervals of scene-painting that I wrote "The Broad Highway," a large portion of it in the great, dismal studio, grimy and rat-haunted, at 38th Street and 10th Avenue, New York City, in which place my work of scene-painting compelled me to pass a great many of my nights and days. For two years every moment I could snatch from other work I gave to my writing, and at the end, sent it out into the world to try its fortune. It was returned from two publishers—The Century Co. and Messrs. Scribner's—with promptitude. Messrs. Dodd, Mead, and Co., declined it as "too long and too English." An actor friend—with the very best intentions—took it with him to Boston, intending to submit it to a firm in that city, but forgot all about it, and brought it back at the end of the year unopened. Then I was minded to burn it—it was cumbersome, and a disappointment—how great only those who have been similarly circumstanced can know. But wiser counsels prevailed, and I decided to send the MS. to my mother, feeling sure that if she, who has ever been—and is still—my severest critic, thought well of it, something might be done with it in England. After carefully reading it, fearing her own judgement might be prejudiced, she gave it to her old friend, Shirley B. Jevons, at that time Editor of the "Sportsman", to whom I subsequently dedicated the book; and he, seeing virtues in it which I fondly hope may be there, it was duly published by Messrs. Sampson Low, Marston, and Co., the only firm it has been submitted to on this side of the Atlantic, and has been most kindly received by the public, both in England and America.

This story was certainly never intended for publication, since it was told by Farnol to his sister Dorothy, in about 1895. In her handwritten memoirs, some 75 years later, she recounts the tale—a true story—as best she could recall, in Jeffery's own words. It comes from the time he was apprenticed to an engineering works in Birmingham, before he had started his writing career; it is highly probable that this is the very first story he ever completed. It had no title, of course, so I have simply called it:

BOOTS

My brother Jeffery was talking to his foreman one day, who noticed that he was looking at his terribly shabby boots, and said to him "I see you're looking at my old boots!" "Yes," my brother said, "I was." I will now continue as though they were talking together:

A day or two later, the foreman came up to me, and said "Jeff, boy, I want to ask you a favour." "Oh?" said I. "Yes," said Bill. "I saw you looking at these boots of mine."

"I was," said I, "for they are a bit the worse for wear, old chap."

"Well, now," said Bill, "I want you to take care of some money for me, to save up to get a new pair of boots I've seen, but they will cost thirty bob, and I shall never be able to save that, so will you hold it for me like a pal?"

"Alright," said I, "I'll ask my old granny to keep it for us. She's a grand old girl, and would do a lot for me!"

So—he saved up every week, until at last he had got the money. Then he said to me "Will you come along with me, Jeff boy, to buy my boots?"

"Alright," said I, so one Saturday off we went into Birmingham, where he had seen the boots in a shop there. While walking along the busy street, we saw a poor wretched man, who looked half-starved, and who had a terribly scarred face, horrible to look at, walking towards us in the gutter, with a few pairs of bootlaces in his hand to sell. As he came abreast of me and Bill, he stared at Bill and in a dreadful hoarse voice said "Bill!" I heard Bill exclaim "My God, Tom, what the hell have you been doing?"

I walked on a little way and left them talking. After a time, Bill caught up with me, and his face was ghastly white, and his eyes glaring. I said "What's up, old chap?"

He made a kind of strangled reply, and I said "Look, we're passing the shop you want to go to for your boots."

"I don't want the bloody boots!" he almost shouted.

"Look here," I said. "You're all upset; here's a pub, come in and have a pint, and tell me what's the matter." So in we went, and he told me—that Tom used to work at the same place as Bill, then Bill said to me "I left, and went to the firm I am with now, and Tom had an accident at the place where he worked, and got badly burnt in the face.

"And now," said Bill, "nobody will give him a job, the bloody swine, and he's starving!"

I didn't speak for a moment or two, and then I said "So you gave him the thirty bob you had saved up for your boots?"

"Well, what else could I do?" he shouted.

I clapped him on the back and "God bless you, Bill, you're a good chap," I said.

When I got home that evening, I was thinking about Bill, and about the poor chap that he had told me about, and presently my dear old granny said to me "You look sad, my dear lad, what is the matter?" So I told her this story about Bill, and his boots, cutting out the bad language.

"Dear, dear," she said, "we must give the poor man some money. How much can we afford, Kizzie? I think—ten shillings, yes, ten shillings!"

So Granny insisted on doing this, and when I went to work the next day, I told the chaps what had happened about Bill, and we had a 'whip round' and collected the rest of the money for his boots. A few nights after, I was going home, and I had brought the money with me that morning. It was a horrible night, pouring with rain, and I caught up with Bill, who was walking on the other side of the road, squelching along in his old boots.

"Bill!" I called out, "here—I've got something for you!", and I crossed the road, and handed him the money.

"For your boots," I said.

He glared at it, then at me, saying "What the bloody hell is this"

"My old Granny, bless her, and some of the chaps at work," I said, and I forced the money into his hand. He couldn't speak, but his look of gratitude was more eloquent than words, as he trudged off through the rain.

And that's the true story of the boots.

I first discovered the existence of this short story, "The Oubliette", through a letter in the files of Farnol's literary agents. Written in 1910, it was from the editor of 'Young's Magazine' in the U.S., and offered Farnol $20 for the story. He subsequently told his agents that he couldn't remember if he'd accepted; they sold the story to George Newnes Limited's 'Grand Magazine' for 15 guineas, where it appeared in February 1913, after he had become famous as the author of 'The Broad Highway'. 'Young's', however, had already published 'The Oubliette' in their March 15, 1912 issue, no doubt cashing in on his popularity as the world's best-selling fiction writer. In fact, it was the 'Young's' publication that Farnol used to obtain his copyright number at the British Museum. Although a great many of Jeffery Farnol's magazine stories appeared in later anthologies, this is the first re-publication of this story since 1913.

THE OUBLIETTE

When Isobel Dering married the Marquis des Tourelles everyone agreed that the match was a most brilliant one, and Isobel had done vastly well for herself—everyone, that is to say, with the exception of Geoffrey Ingleby. But then, to be sure, Ingleby was prejudiced, for he had pursued her unremittingly, desperately, to the last.

Of course, Ingleby had never possessed the ghost of a chance from the outset, and this for three reasons: First, Ingleby was by no means rich; second, Isobel's father was more than rich; and third, but by no means least, Isobel's mother was ambitious. It is true that Isobel had a ring that Ingleby had once given her, a trumpery thing which she treasured from all eyes, and shed many tears over, but, as has been said, her mother had ambitions—also she possessed a chin. So, in due course, the marriage took place, with the World and His Wife to look smilingly on and to fill the bride's ears with good wishes and warm congratulations, and everyone to bow the knee to the beautiful young Marquise—always excepting Ingleby, of course. Upon the day she married, Ingleby disappeared from his regular haunts. Some said that he had gone West; some opined that he was down South; and others that he had fled to the Continent. Be that as it may, from that very hour London saw Geoffrey Ingleby no more.

The Château des Tourelles, where the Marquis took his bride, is a grey, old, embattled pile that frowns grimly down upon a smiling landscape of vine-clad slopes and laughing streams, as it has done since it was built, eight hundred years ago. As the château had, in days gone by, possessed an evil reputation, and been avoided by the terrified peasantry, so in these more modern times, more especially since the young Marquis's advent, it had become infamous in other ways, so that the peasants avoided it still. And yet there was one, a great broad-shouldered, loose-limbed fellow named François, who had got himself work in the château gardens, and who, sometimes, eked out his slender earnings by showing inquisitive tourists over the more ancient parts of the château, such as the dungeons, the torture-chamber, and the *oubliette*.

"*Voyons, messieurs!*" he would say, regarding this last, "I turn this rusty lever—so, and—*voila!*" While he spoke there would come the groan and creak of rusty iron, and in that moment the great flagstone set in the midst of the floor would fall away before their eyes, turning upon itself until it sloped down into blackness below, leaving a yawning cavity in the floor, through which rose an odour, acrid and noisome with decay.

"Hark!" he would say, holding up a warning finger, "there are rats down there—hundreds, thousands of them. If you do but listen you will hear them squeak, and scamper down there in the darkness. And they are big, these rats—for I have seen them—bigger than any other rats in all the country hereabouts, for behold now, their great-great grandfathers lived high, and fed full when the world was younger. Oh! I tell you, *messieurs*, these rusty bolts and levers were kept smooth and well-oiled once upon a time. They called these things *oubliettes*—places of forgetfulness, *messieurs*, for once the great stone yonder had closed upon a man he was soon forgotten and out of mind. But, for the rats, look you, they live on down there, as you may hear, and sometimes it seems to me, *messieurs*, that they are waiting—but, should you ask me for what, or whom?" and here François would smile in his russet beard, and shrug his broad shoulders. So the levers would creak and groan once more, the flagstone would rise into place, he would accept the proffered *pourboire* with a murmur of thanks, and show the silenced tourists out of the dungeon.

To-day, however, François was busied clipping and shaping the high privet hedge that bordered the rose garden. Yet, as he worked, his glance was often turned toward the pale, beautiful face of her who sat nearby among the roses, staring away to the blue of the distant hills. But presently, as if attracted by the persistence of his gaze, she looked up suddenly, and saw him. Now, as their eyes met, her lips parted, a wave of burning colour suffused the pallor of her cheek, and her white hand clenched upon the arm of her chair. But, quick as it had come, the eager light was gone from her eyes, and she turned away to stare listlessly at the distant hills once more.

The roses bent and swayed, nodding slumberously one to another; butterflies wheeled and hovered, and no sound disturbed the dreamy stillness of the afternoon save the sharp click, click of the gardener's shears. The Marquise sat chin in hand, as one buried deep in thought. And the sun made a glory of her hair, but, alas! It could not light up the depths of her sombre eyes; and, despite the nodding roses, and the butterflies, and the beauty of the world around her, she sighed drearily, and once her eyes brimmed with scalding tears, and the gardener, watching her, stood rigid, and the click, click of the shears ceased. Whereupon she turned again and, meeting his eyes, drew herself up proudly, and beckoned to him with a disdainful hand. Obedient to her summons, he came.

"Why do you stand there and stare at me?"

He looked down and shrugged his shoulders, murmuring in his beard: "Madame will, perhaps, pardon my so great liberty."

"Who are you?" she demanded, her eyes suddenly intent.

"I am François, the gardener," he answered.

"I haven't seen you—before."

"That is because madame leads a life so secluded."

"How long have you been here—at the château?"

"Six months, madame."

Once more she turned to look across the valley; but, even as François moved away, she spoke, though without looking at him: "Were you—born here—in these parts?"

"I was born, madame, over yonder!" and he pointed away into the hazy distance.

"And your name is—François?" said she, with her eyes still averted, while her white fingers were drumming nervously upon the arm of her chair.

"Yes, madame—François."

"You are the man, I think, who shows tourists over the château—the dungeons, and the *oubliette?*"

"Yes, madame."

"Take me there."

"Madame wishes to see the—*oubliette?*"

"Yes."

"But the stairs are dusty, and hard to climb, and madame—"

"—Wishes to see the *oubliette,*" said she, rising. "Come, take me there, François."

So, perforce, François bowed, and went before her through the gardens, all unconscious of the eyes behind him, wide and eager, that watched the swing of his broad shoulders, his long, easy stride, and how the hair grew in little close curls upon his bronzed neck.

By devious ways he brought her to the Great Tower that frowned above them, grim and forbidding, and went on before her down a narrow stone stair, pausing at the bottom to find and light a battered lantern, and so, down more steps and into a dungeon lit by a little grill high up in the massive wall.

"This is the dungeon of the *oubliette*," said he, pausing and holding up the lantern, for the light from the grill was very dim, despite the glory of the afternoon sun outside. "Yonder madame can see for herself the midmost flagstone, the large one—that is the mouth of the *oubliette*."

"Open it," said she, "let me see how it works."

Slowly, almost unwillingly, François set down the lantern; the levers creaked beneath his hand, the flagstone fell away, and the mouth of the *oubliette* yawned black and hideous before her. Slowly, very slowly, she approached, and looked down into the noisome depths. Her breath caught with a gasp, and then, as he watched her, François saw that she had closed her eyes—she took a sudden step forward; but in that instant she was swept back, and caught up by two powerful arms. And, lying in that close embrace, she glanced up through her lashes into the face of the gardener that was bent down so near to her own, and in that moment her bosom rose with a long, fluttering sigh. Then he had released her, suddenly, almost roughly; but there was a smile upon her lips as she leaned back against the wall while he turned to close the *oubliette*.

"Why, François," said she at last, but not looking at him now, "did you think I was—going to—fall?"

"Madame was perhaps overcome with giddiness," he muttered, and took up his lantern to light her out of the dungeon. Now at the foot of the dark stair she stopped.

"François," said she, "you were right, the stair is very steep, and difficult to climb—give me your hand."

And thus it befell that her hand was yet in his when they presently emerged into the sunshine above.

Happening to glance down at those slender white fingers ere he released them, he saw, upon one of them, a ring; surely a very trumpery affair to grace the hand of so proud a lady.

"François," said she suddenly, "what is the matter?" But François only muttered in his beard, and turned upon his heel.

But now, as they crossed the gardens together, her cheek was pale no longer, and the look of dreary hopelessness was gone from her eyes.

A servant approached, bearing a letter, and the gardener noticed that the hand she stretched out for it was trembling as it had not done a moment ago; therefore, as he fell to his clipping again, he watched her under his brows while she read the words of the letter, and he saw the loathing in her look, heard it quiver in her voice as she turned to the waiting servant.

"Your master will be here tonight with a visitor—see that rooms are prepared for them." As the servant bowed and withdrew she crumpled the letter in her hand, and stood awhile looking across the valley. Then she turned, and went slow-footed along the winding walk, until she had vanished among the roses. But the gardener's sharp eyes espied the crumpled letter where it had fallen beside the path, and, picking it up, he smoothed it out, and his thick brows met in an evil frown as he read:

MA BELLE,—My money troubles accumulate. Without our friend de Marsac I am lost, bankrupt, and utterly ruined. He is as eager to meet you as ever. I am bringing him with me to-night. Let your reception of him be gracious, for he is our only salvation.—thine, ETIENNE.

Indeed, the face of François, the gardener, was terrible to see, as his strong, brown fingers tore and wrenched the letter to pieces.

II.

"Isobel," said the Marquis, kissing his wife's hand in his pretty, graceful way, "you remember our good friend de Marsac, whom we met at Monte Carlo last year?"

She rose to greet the visitor, but her cheeks burned at the look in de Marsac's sleepy eyes, and she shivered at the touch of de Marsac's soft, white hand.

"I trust madame has not quite forgotten me?" he said in his slow, gently-modulated voice that was so hatefully like a caress. Forgotten him! She grew hot with shame when she remembered this man's bold and persistent pursuit of her scarcely a year ago. She had complained to her husband, then—but he, careless or indifferent, and busied with his own pleasures, had laughed her fears to scorn. And now, as she faced de Marsac, all her old dread and loathing of the man returned. Surely Etienne would see for himself at last, would know that her fears were not altogether baseless; he had but to read the look in de Marsac's eyes. Surely, surely her husband must see it for himself. She turned towards him almost appealingly, then stood chilled with unexpected dread, for the Marquis had crossed to the door, and, with a gay, laughing excuse he went out—leaving them together.

She stood for a moment staring at the door which had just closed behind her husband, then sank into a chair, gazing blindly out of the open window, and deaf to the soft murmur of de Marsac's voice, for, with a sickening rush, had come a realisation of the hateful truth. And now she burned with shame, and now she trembled with a bodily fear; but while she sat there striving to quell the tremor of her limbs, her down-bent gaze encountered a ring upon her finger, that same small ring that was so very plain and trumpery.

"Madame is *distrait?*" de Marsac was saying.

She lifted her head suddenly, the rich blood mantled in her cheek, and her eyes were like stars.

"*Distrait?*—but no—I am very well—oh, very well!" and she laughed as she spoke.

De Marsac, leaning near her, talked of trivialities; the weather, the newest opera, the latest fashionable scandal, but all the while his sleepy eyes enveloped her, from the slender foot beneath her gown to the crowning glory of her hair, and ever and anon his teeth gleamed between the parted crimson of his lips. Moreover, there was in his treatment of her a subtle familiarity, an air of easy assurance in his every gesture that she found it difficult to endure.

She rose suddenly, and crossing to the open window, stood there, leaning out into the fragrant evening. De Marsac's eyes devoured the beauty of her averted face and the round white column of her throat; but she was watching a tall figure that passed slowly among the roses.

"Are you not very lonely here, so far from Paris, and life, and laughter?" inquired de Marsac suddenly.

"No," she answered, her eyes still intent upon the shadowy form below. "In Paris I was always lonely."

"Isobel!"

She started beneath the touch of his fingers upon her bare arm, and sprang away from him.

"Monsieur de Marsac!" she exclaimed.

"I startled you!" said he; "pray forgive me!" But she turned from him disdainfully. "Alas!" he sighed, "I fear that you have yet to learn that I am the most devoted of your friends—Isobel."

"I hate you, Monsieur de Marsac!"

"That," said he, shaking his head gently, "that is most unfortunate, both for me and for—your husband!"

"What do you mean?" she asked breathlessly, struck by something in his tone and look.

"I mean that the Marquis is in most desperate straits—financially—his credit is quite exhausted—his social position is in jeopardy—"

"Well?"

"I could—perhaps—avert the threatened disaster."

"Well?"

"If—you bid me, Isobel!"

"I?"

"You!" There was a quiver of eagerness in his voice. "Say but the word, Isobel, or let me but read it in your eyes, and my wealth, my influence—my very self are yours to do with as you will."

"And—my—husband?"

De Marsac shrugged his shoulders.

"Etienne was never—quite a fool!"

She put out a hand, leaning as if for support against a chair-back, then, suddenly, swiftly, she turned and fled from the room, and down the long corridor beyond.

But as de Marsac watched her go the smile of confidence was still upon his lips.

III.

"So you say she actually ran away and left you?" said the Marquis, sipping thoughtfully at his liqueur. "My faith, how she does—hate you, de Marsac!" And there was more than a suspicion of malice in the Marquis's smile as he spoke.

"So much the better!" nodded de Marsac. "A little hatred, my dear Etienne, is occasionally deliciously piquant!"

"And pray, why should she have flown away from such a *preux chevalier* as yourself?" inquired the Marquis, after another thoughtful sip.

"I ventured to speak to her of your present financial—er—difficulty," smiled de Marsac.

"That she already knows," sighed the Marquis, "at least—to some extent—so it couldn't have been that altogether."

"I ventured also," pursued de Marsac, "to assure her that your credit might yet be saved, your—ah—rather numerous liabilities met, and—disposed of—"

"Conditionally, of course?" murmured the Marquis.

"Precisely, my dear fellow!"

"And then," sighed the Marquis, "she—ran away?"

"Exactly, my dear fellow."

The Marquis emptied his glass, lighted a cigarette, and rising, crossed to the window.

"de Marsac," said he, speaking with his back to his companion, "do you—mean it?"

"I do, Etienne—on my honour!"

As he spoke, de Marsac's eyes were, all at once, sleepy no longer.

"You know the amount of my liabilities?"

"To a franc!"

"Then you know that, without your aid, I am ruined—utterly—irretrievably?"

"My dear Etienne, no man but a fool would consider himself ruined or bankrupt while he has so priceless an asset as you possess."

"And—she ran away!" murmured the Marquis. His sharp white teeth bit down through the cigarette, and he tossed it out of the window. "Eight hundred thousand francs!" he said, as if to himself.

"Nine!" smiled de Marsac. "Nine!"

The Marquis turned, stretched himself, and sauntered to the door; upon the threshold he paused, for de Marsac had risen.

"You are—going, Etienne?"

"To teach Madame la Marquise that a wife's duty may sometimes induce her not to—run away."

The Marquis smiled, nodded, and went out, closing the door behind him.

The cigar slipped from de Marsac's fingers and lay neglected at his feet, and the smile that curved his satyr's mouth was not pleasant to behold. In a little while he crossed to the open window and leaned out into the cool night. Now, as he stood thus, it almost seemed that a dark figure moved away, and was lost in the shadows of the garden.

Meanwhile, the Marquis des Tourelles took his way by vaulted passages and echoing corridors, his wife's apartments being in another wing of the château; and, as he went, he hummed the lilt of a song, for it seemed to him that his way was become smooth and straight, the incubus of impending ruin and disaster was about to be lifted from his shoulders—thus, as he went, he hummed gaily to himself.

But, all at once, the Marquis found himself caught in a powerful grip; his cry for help was choked back in his throat, he was swung round against the wall, and the cold rim of a revolver was pressed against his temple.

"Come with me!" said François, the gardener, speaking through shut teeth, "utter a word—cry out, and you are a dead man—come!"

So, perforce, the Marquis obeyed those compelling hands that guided him along unfamiliar passage-ways, and down sudden flights of steps, through dim, unused chambers, and out at last into the velvet blackness of the night. On they went through the cool, sweet perfume of the roses, until they reached a great and massive door that yawned upon its hinges. And now they descended more stairs, down and down until they reached a chamber with walls and floor of stone. Upon an empty barrel, near by, stood a lantern with a guttering candle whose uncertain, flickering light filled the place with ever-moving shadows. Here they stopped, and the Marquis, released from those gripping hands, found voice in an outburst of passionate abuse. But, of a sudden, his breath caught, the angry words died upon his lips, for by the uncertain gleam of the lantern he beheld sundry cranks and levers in a niche near by, and, turning his eyes in a certain direction, he started back, shivering, from that hideous, yawning chasm. From this, with an effort, he dragged his gaze to look upon the man beside him, the man who stared back at him, and in whose relentless eyes he saw the purpose of their coming.

"My God!" he cried, "have you brought me here to murder me?"

"No," answered François, "to fight!"

"Are you mad?" exclaimed the Marquis.

"No, Marquis," returned the gardener; "but I loved your wife, two years ago, and to-night I know the vile thing you would do. And so, unless you get the better of me, I mean to throw you down there—to the rats, Monsieur le Marquis!"

As he spoke, he produced two broad-bladed knives from his pocket, one of which he held out to the Marquis.

"I am bigger than you—this may even up matters a little. Come, take it, take it! So, are you ready? Then fight—for your life!"

The candle-flame flickered to and fro, filling the place with shadows that leaped and danced and writhed hideously together, but from that flurry of tangled shapes came the stamp and shuffle of quick-moving feet, the clash of steel, and the pant and hiss of breath drawn through teeth close-set in mortal combat; and ever and always, those writhing, twisting shapes drew nearer and nearer to the gaping void in the floor. All at once there rose a gurgling, choking cry—a strangled cry; then, far down below, a splash, and immediately the air rang with the squealing of the rusty iron levers, and the yawning chasm in the floor gaped no longer.

But now came the sound of fast-falling feet upon the stair without—the door was thrown open, and the Marquise sped across the chamber and caught the great lever in desperate hands; than, all at once, she grew rigid, a great sobbing cry burst from her lips, and she threw out her arms.

"Geoffrey—I'm afraid! Oh, Geoffrey, save me—save me!"

Now, in that moment, even as his hands were outstretched to clasp her—even as his radiant eyes looked down into hers, from the depths below, piercing the stones beneath their feet, came a long, soul-shaking scream that rose higher and higher, and so died away and was gone.

She had covered her ears against the horror of it, but, reading the truth within his eyes, cowered back to the wall, and, sinking down, fell, and lay outstretched at his feet.

Then François, the gardener, lifted her in his arms, and hid her face against his breast, and bore her from the chamber and up the stair, out into the dewy freshness of the night.

* * * * * * * * * * *

Monsieur de Marsac, grown impatient for the return of the Marquis, had turned him again to the window. Thus he was presently aware of the pant of an automobile somewhere near by among the shadows, that, as he listened, grew rapidly fainter and fainter until it had hummed itself away into the distance.

And thus it was that the beautiful Marquise vanished from the Château des Tourelles, even as one Geoffrey Ingleby had disappeared from his haunts in London two years before.

After the end of the Great War, the Industrial Welfare Society, founded in England by the Rev.(later Sir) Robert Hyde, was attempting to bridge the gap between management and 'men'—a gap so wide as to be almost inconceivable today. Prince Albert, Duke of York, George V's second son (later King George VI), was the Society's first president. Together, he and Hyde came up with the idea of bringing together, in an annual week-long camp, boys just leaving the great public schools (presumably future management) and boys already working in factories. These became known as the Duke of York's Camps, and ran from 1921 until the start of World War II; they received a great deal of publicity, because of the royal connection, and certainly helped the work of the Industrial Welfare Society. Jeffery Farnol was invited by the Prince's secretary to attend the very first camp in 1921 and to write an exclusive article about it for the "Daily Telegraph", a popular upper-class newspaper. This article appeared on September 5, 1921, beside stories about the crashes of two British airships, the R38 and R39, and a call by Prince Hirohito of Japan for "lasting peace".

NEW ROMNEY CAMP

One of the very few good things resultant from the late hateful war was the spirit of comradeship it evoked among all sorts and conditions of men; its very horrors taught them to know and, consequently, to respect and have faith in each other. Peasant and prince, noble and labourer, clerk and artisan, found each other out in these evil days, whence grew a new sympathy and fellowship, which it was hoped would endure.

But, alas, this great, good thing seems to have been more or less lost of late in the welter of industrial troubles. And yet, can anything great and good perish utterly? Surely not!

The Duke of York, who is mightily interested in all progressive movements, has turned his attention towards the coming generation rather than the present; to which end he formed a camp at New Romney, in Kent, where he lately brought together 400 of our future citizens (between the ages of 16 and 18), boys from many of the great industrial centres and famous public schools.

And a wonderfully mixed company they were; for here were Scots from o'er the Border, lads from the black squads of Clyde and Tyne and the humming workshops of Birmingham, Manchester and Sheffield; here were young textile workers, boys from the mines, others from the docks, with lads from Eton, Harrow, Wellington, Tonbridge, and many another famous old school. And a truly impossible company they might have seemed to the casual observer, perhaps; but the Prince trusted that the close association of camp life, and more particularly that love of sport and fair play, which is a part of every true Briton's psychology, might teach these boys, despite all differences of speech, manner, and outward seeming, to understand and justly appreciate each other. And never was faith more triumphantly vindicated.

For six days I have lived with these boys, eating with them, bathing with them, watching, and (often enough) sharing in their games, and, notwithstanding the healthy discomforts incidental to camp life, I enjoyed every moment of it. I would say that these future citizens of ours are worthy of their stock and the land that bred them; indeed, if they be truly representative of their fellows (as I believe them to be), I, for one, have no fear for the future of the race as regards bodily and mental fitness.

As some collect butterflies and postage stamps, I collect impressions of men and things, particularly the former, and my impressions gathered during these six days are so many and varied that I can here set down but few.

The Game of Life

And first, the Camp Chief (he who was responsible for the excellent organisation and particularly for the wonderful system of games), a slender man, of no great size, of expression gently resolute, austerely kind, inexorably calm, quick to cope with all emergencies and never at a loss, whom all gladly obeyed because of the confidence he inspired, one who the Four Hundred cheered lustily whenever occasion offered. So there stands our Camp Chief, as I remember him, with his face suggestive of knights-errant, resolute martyrs, and prophets quietly determined to be heard; and long may he live, for he is, in very truth, a man.

And here I can do no better than set forth his rules for playing that game, the greatest of all, which is the game of life.

1. Don't play foul.
2. Don't chuck up the sponge.
3. Go all out to win.
4. Play for your *side,* not for your *self.*

Also must I mention his two able lieutenants, so full of zeal, sympathy, and understanding, yet each so vastly different from the other; then there was the doctor, the merriest dying man (snatched from the grave by his own indomitable will) it has ever been my joy to know. There were the section leaders, a notable company, numbering amongst them a V.C. and two M.C.'s—in ordinary life, works' managers, schoolmasters, social workers, padres, ex-Army and naval officers—men whose memory I treasure, one and all, and of whom I may write more—but in another place, for here I would hasten on to tell of this great scheme, with the reasons for its wonderful success, to the which end I must briefly describe something of the inner organisation of this camp.

Firstly, there were no hard and fast rules; no scurrying about of contumacious corporals and the like hectoring bodies full of peremptory orders; yet the routine of camp duties went on orderly and well, since each boy was trusted to play the game, and be worthy of his leaders, his fellows, and himself. Nor was this expectation disappointed in one single instance.

The camp was divided into five groups of eighty boys, called respectively, "Red", "White", "Blue", "Green", and "Yellow." These were each sub-divided into four sections thus:

  Red   White   Blue
 A.B.C.D. E.F.G.H. I.J.K.L. &c

each of these sections being in charge of a section leader. Each group had its own sleeping-hut, thus fostering section and group spirit. Each group had its allotted playing-ground for the competitions; each competition being between the same two sections throughout: A. always competing with B., C. with D., and so on.

The Boys

And now—the boys. For the first few hours they were shy and constrained (as is the way of your true Britons the world over), but with rare sagacity and judgement, their several leaders preserved an attitude of masterly inaction, leaving the boys to discover each other in their own way as best they might. And it worked—for next morning the long breakfast tables rang with the cheery babel of voices where the various sections discussed their chances in the impending tournament; shyness and restraint vanished, and each section became, as it were, a small community bonded together by sport and a growing good-fellowship, each boy eager for achievement, not so much to show his individual prowess as for the honour of his section.

That morning also I was installed Scavenger-in-Chief to the camp, with a sanitary squad of twenty boys to collect waste-paper, &c., and generally tidy up. Forth we went accordingly, myself between a somewhat dour-looking lad from Renfrew and a debonair, smiling boy from Wellington.

"An' what'll I dae wi' a' this, sir?" inquires Renfrew, showing me his load of odds and ends.

"I think buckets would be a rather topping scheme, sir," suggests Wellington.

"A notable idea," quoth I. "Buckets it is!" Whereupon, off went Renfrew and Wellington, chatting together like the friends they were to become.

"Hi sye, sir!" exclaimed one of my company, securing the derelict and weather-beaten cigarette box we had both dived for, "These 'ere blokes from the swell schools don't seem s' very different t' us blokes w'en y' gits t' know 'em, do they?"

"Why, no," said I, "we're all much the same if you dig deep enough."

Our scavenging done, we presently joined the others and strolled down to the beach for the morning dip; and watching the flash of these white young bodies as they ran hallooing blithely across the sands, or sported in the water, I must needs think of *"Sartor Resartus"* and of how true it was that oft-times "clothes make the man."

Later, in a quiet corner of the wind-swept playing-field I came upon a small, hoarse-voiced person in preposterous trousers and monstrous peaked cap walking between two seniors, whose crested blazers, and immaculate shorts proclaimed them public school boys beyond a peradventure, and all three in profound converse.

Was it sartorial oddities they discussed, think you? Not so! Our two immaculates were instructing their be-capped and trousered "man" precisely how he must "take off" in the hop, skip, and jump, that he might do himself and his side justice in the forthcoming event.

Yes, indeed, that thing we call "sport" was up and stirring, and every lesser consideration was clean forgotten; boys of the schools and lads of the factories went side by side into the field to do their utmost for the honour of their section.

Among the public-school boys were many promising athletes, captains of their various houses or their several cricket and football teams; therefore, that all might be as equal as possible, among these events was neither cricket or football; in their stead other games had been devised—tests of pluck, skill, and endurance, such as: relay and weight-carrying races, obstacle races, tugs-of-war, land-boat races, and the ancient game of stool-ball. Many other carefully-thought-out competitions were there, in which each and every boy had his chance to add to the total score of his side. Thus, was a lad hopelessly beaten in any contest, marks were awarded, nevertheless, if he but did his best and finished gamely; and few were there who gave up, since one might score a mark for his side, even if he walked home, so long as he got there somehow.

An Obstacle Race

I have mentioned the "obstacle race". This was a particularly grueling affair of benches that had to be alternatively dived under and leapt over in the one direction, and wriggled or squirmed under coming back. And great joy was it to one and all, despite bruises, scratched elbows, and bloody knees. K section had finished the event (and I cheering myself hoarse) when their leader challenged me to race him over the same skin-abrading course for half-a-crown. Off came our coats forthwith, and amid a deafening but cheery clamour we dived and leapt and squirmed together; and when I eventually staggered across the mark, a bare winner, it was worth the smart of my grazed and bleeding shin to hear the roar of acclaim that greeted me; the years rolled away and I was all boy again as hands patted my back or reached to grip mine, and from that moment I was of their honourable company, and a brother of the Four Hundred. This I mention because thenceforth they hailed me as one of them selves, and I was enabled to see more of them, and at a closer range, than I had ever deemed possible. That same hour a boy from the engineering shops of the Midlands honoured me by desiring to take my photograph; on this wise:

"Hey, Jeff, will yer lemme take yer picktcha?"

After him came Harrow or Marlborough with "May I do the same, sir—I mean, Jeff?"

The last event held was a mile and a half cross-country race—very rough going, with plenty of fence, hedge, and ditch, which, owing to their week's training, held no terrors for the Four Hundred, and was accomplished in eight minutes and a few seconds. My chief memory of this race is of a small urchin who came in among the very last, a strange, fiercely-determined little figure, hatless and shoeless, that he might run the better, but in a pair of remarkably baggy trousers girt about him by a very wide pair of braces and a belt; on he came, far in the rear, but determined to make a good fight for it none the less; panting and blowing he ran, elbows well in, small face fiercely set and resolute, trousers flip-flopping, but never faltering in his stride. And as they watched this small, lonely figure, who, though so hopelessly outdistanced, maintained a spirit yet unconquered, the boys about me broke into a cheer, like the true sportsmen they were—a cheer that swelled ever louder, as, with a final desperate spurt, the flopping trousers passed the line, and their wearer tumbled in a panting heap, only to be picked up and borne shoulder-high, bashfully a-grin, to be clapped and cheered because he had done his best to play the game. And indeed, talking of this, I saw more of the true, clean spirit of sport during these six days than in all my life, I do verily believe.

Duke of York's Visit

When the Duke of York came to greet them, they met him with no undue shyness, no servile truckling, but, bright-eyed and with heads aloft, they hearkened to his manly words with grave and eager attention;

and when he had done, cheered him to the echo full-heartedly, and I think the Prince was touched by their unaffected loyalty and gratitude.

So sped these halcyon days, full of sun and wind and laughter, with games vigorously contested on the field, bare-limbed scampers across smooth sands, joyous plunges through curling breakers, shouts, merriment, and good fellowship—such an atmosphere as no true cynic could possibly have endured for a single moment—and, as evening fell, back, light-treading, to supper.

The meal ended, off and away to the camp's own private cinema and the concert, produced almost entirely by camp "talent", and every item (choruses included) cheered to the joyous echo. The long programme worked through, came a hymn, sung right heartily, and prayers as short as they were eloquent, every head reverently bowed except my own (I who must be forever gathering impressions) until the camp chief's clear voice pronounced the final Amen.

And now at every door—Biscuits! (four apiece and of the best), and so away to quarters for the night, but not for sleep yet awhile. Faint and far would presently steal the drone of bag-pipes, weirdly sad, and then a yelp, a shout, a distant cheering; and hasting forth into the night I would behold dim figures that flitted in the surrounding gloom, would hear the swift patter of feet, a thudding of hearty blows, where pillows whirled and swung and the battle raged; until blows, shouts, and cheering were drowned suddenly in the snarl of the pipes where the Scots rushed to the fray. So, one and all, they reeled and swayed and smote each other cheerily—these Britons of factory and school, until, across the dim square, stole the plaintive notes of the "Last Post"—that wistfully mournful appeal that few Britons I think may hear unmoved because of yesterday. And so would come silence and presently sleep, as sound as it was sweet.

But Saturday dawned at last, and with it a pervading and wistful regret that the week was over, and the camp so soon to break up—a feeling that affected us one and all. Fortune send I may know such again, for this camp is, I believe, to become an institution. And who shall say that by the understanding and comradeship that are necessarily born in such camps as this, may not come that great, good thing, which shall one day banish the Spectre of War, and bring in its stead a knowledge and fellowship that shall endure among all men soever.

Here is but a dream, perhaps; well, let the cynic howl—but dreams are the inspiration to action. And there was once a Man who dreamed a new heaven and a new earth, and died like a malefactor. But His dream lives yet, and will live on for ever.

Although this story does not really meet the criteria of never having been published in book form, since it appears in 'A Matter of Business' published in 1940, I include it here because it differs from the published version; differs in the way the spoken is not the same as the written word. Strangely, I happened to hear this actual broadcast; although I enjoyed Farnol's work, I was not then the collector I later became (I was just 21). But I can still hear his voice as he told it, almost as if he were sitting across the fireplace from me in the other armchair, and recalling the incident from memory; he was a natural storyteller, and must have been a fascinating dinner companion. This is from a transcription of the broadcast; I have made one or two alterations in the actual transcript, where it was apparent that the transcriber had misheard Farnol's speech.

A TALE OF MY GRANDFATHER

from a broadcast by Jeffery Farnol on the British Broadcasting Corporation Light Programme "Tellers of Tales", August 6, 1951

Announcer: This is the BBC Light Programme, and the British Forces Network in Germany. For our story tonight in the series, TELLERS OF TALES, we took a recording van down to Eastbourne last week to the home of Jeffery Farnol. Mr Farnol is in the throes of writing a new historical romance, but he took time off to record this story for us which he told straight into the microphone without rehearsal, and without script: A TALE OF MY GRANDFATHER

Farnol: I'm going to tell you a story, our family ghost story. It is the tale of my maternal grandfather, John Jeffery, a Cornishman who died a hero's death saving two people from a fire. He saved them—oh yes!—but died the following week aged only 44. They called me after him, John Jeffery, and I am proud to bear such a name.

And now—now to the story, which I will tell as nearly as possible as did his adoring wife, my blessed grandmother, a tale she loved to tell, and which she did regularly every Christmas, and which we loved to hear.

"My dears," she would say, glancing round upon us with a look that gathered and held our attention, "your dear grandfather was one of the handsomest of men, with a pair of the most beautiful black whiskers. And he was a dandy also! I remember when we journeyed to Cornwall on our honeymoon he wore a flowered satin waistcoat and a pair of lavender—hum!—unmentionables, strapped under his insteps so tightly that when he sat down he was quite unable to bend his knees. But at that time no properly dressed gentleman ever possibly could.

"Well, upon a day, my dears, we found ourselves at Bodmin in Cornwall, and he said to me: 'Mrs Jeffery, ma'am, by your good leave I will walk across Bodmin Moor to visit my old friend John Penberthy, whom I haven't seen since we were at college together.'

"Oh, but John," said I, "dearest Mr Jeffery, 'tis such a hot day, and such a long way, and you know it's said the moor is haunted. If you must go, do take the carriage, or ride a horse.

"But no, he insisted he must walk. Well, my dears, I packed him a nice little luncheon, sandwiches, and a flask of wine; and he carried also a small—what they called then a 'pocket pistol' which was a little sort of a shooter, because in those days the roads were still very dangerous, and away he went.

Well, he came to the moor, and he walked and he walked, and he began to get very tired, and it was very hot and dusty. And presently he began to think: 'What an idiot I was to walk on such a hot day and with so much dust,' and he began to look around for a place where he might sit down in the shade and take his morning meal, his luncheon. Well, he walked and he walked, and presently in the distance there sure enough was an old ruin, casting a shadow, so he walked on until he came to this, and he sat down in the shadow of this old wall, and he undid his knapsack, and he undid his flask, and he began to eat his luncheon.

"And as he ate, he looked up the road, and he looked down the road, but there was no-one in sight. In all that vast expanse there was not a soul to be seen, and he said: 'Surely, surely, I am the world's biggest fool to walk on such a day—nobody else has done such a silly thing.' And he went on eating his luncheon. And presently, my dears, he looked down the road again and then he stared because there in the distance was a solitary wayfarer, and he thought: 'Good gracious, there is another fool in the world. Here is another man braving the dust and the heat,' and he went on eating his luncheon.

"And when he looked again, your grandfather was very astonished. He opened those grey eyes of his and stared very hard because to his amazement, that distant figure was very near now, so very near that he wondered how in the world that man could have travelled so far in so short a time. He was so near that your dear grandfather was enabled to see that he was dressed for riding—in white, I believe they called them buckskins and top boots and spurs. He had an old flat hat on his head, and with every step he took his feet jingled his spurs and put up little puffs of dust because he was dragging them as though he was very tired, and at the same time, with every slow dragging stop, his head, in that peculiar hat, rolled from one shoulder to the other in a very peculiar manner.

"Well, your grandfather watched his approach, and then began to think: 'Dear me, I'm staring very hard. If he sees me staring he'll wonder what I'm doing, why I should stare,' so he didn't. He didn't stare. He went on eating his luncheon. But presently he heard the spurs jingle nearer and nearer, and he glanced up, and that strange traveller had paused right opposite your grandfather, made a right about turn like a soldier, and had come striding up to him, and thrust out his hand.

"Well, my dears, your grandfather was a very brave man: he was a man who dared do anything, and he said: 'Well, sir, I don't know you, but if you care to be friends, I—' and then he looked up; and then, my dears, he was amazed and shocked because this strange being had no face! No features whatever! Beneath the shadow of that hat there was only a mist. However, your grandfather being, as I say, such a very valiant gentleman, reached out and grasped that almost pleading hand.

He was seized in the grip of a giant, pulled and whirled up through the air, crashed down on the other side of the road, heard a thundering roar, and looked, and saw nothing but dust. There he sat, or lay, almost insensible. But the dust slowly cleared, and so did your grandfather's sight and brain. And he looked, and where he had been sitting there was nothing but a mountain of old bricks and stones. They had buried his hat and had buried his knapsack, and had buried his walking stick. He knew that if he had been sitting there he himself would have been buried and killed. So he looked around to find his preserver and thank him; but my dears, there was nobody.

"Then your grandfather pulled out his watch—the gold hunter, John," said she to me, "which some day will be yours." And my dear hearers, between you and me, I never got it. I never shall.

"However, he pulled out his watch, and he looked at it. He opened the case and he looked at it, and it was stopped. And it had stopped at two minutes past one, and do what he could, he could not start it again. Well, after he'd got over his shock, without his hat, and without his knapsack, and without his walking stick, he got up to his feet and he started across the moor.

"As evening fell, and the sun went down, he reached a little village—there was nobody about! The street was deserted, so he walked up that quiet, echoing street, until he reached a little inn, or alehouse. That being the only one in sight, he walked in. There was nobody to see, so he drew a coin from his pocket and he rapped loudly on the bar or counter. But nobody came! Then he stood still and he listened, and from somewhere not very far off he heard a murmur of voices. So your grandfather, being as I say an intrepid gentleman, lifted the counter and walked down that passage until he came to a certain door beyond which were the voices.

"So he rapped on that door, he opened that door, and he stepped into the room, and he saw four gentleman seated at a table, and one of these was dressed in clerical garb. And your grandfather said: 'Gentlemen, you must excuse my interruption, but I have just walked across the moor, I'm exceedingly tired, and I'm very thirsty and hungry, and I desire some refreshment. I've come all this way to see an old friend of mine who lives, I think, somewhere hereabouts—Squire John Penberthy.'"

My dears, there was a moment of rather awful silence, and then the clergyman, who turned out to be the Vicar, looked up at him and said: 'My dear sir, you may see your friend, our Squire, but alas not in life. He's lying in the next room. This morning he was riding a young horse, and he put it at fence, and it tripped, and fell with him; and before he could rise it kicked him full in the face and killed him very dreadfully. Here, sir, are his effects, his gold watch, his purse and his pocket book.'"

"Then, my dears, your grandfather leaned over the table and looked at that watch. And it had stopped at exactly two minutes past one. Then your grandfather turned, and he looked at the assembled company, and he said very solemnly: 'Gentleman, a miracle has happened. I believe most surely that in the moment of his dying, my dear old friend came to me in the middle of Bodmin Moor and saved my life.'"

Well, then our blessed old grandmother would pause, and she'd look around upon us again, and she'd say: "And so, my dears, tonight when you go up to bed, say a small prayer for poor John Penberthy who died so many years ago, because had it not been for him, *you* would none of you have been here."

Announcer: Well, that was Jeffery Farnol telling his story A TALE OF MY GRANDFATHER. It was recorded. Next week's teller of tales will be NIGEL BALCHIN.

In 1921, the fight for the Heavyweight Championship of the World, between Jack Dempsey of the U.S. and Georges Carpentier of France created a great deal of excitement in both Europe and the States. Newspapers were in hot competition to cover the event; the 'Daily Mail', at that time England's (and the world's) most popular newspaper, decided they would not only send an additional boxing expert to augment reports from their regular sporting writer, but also engage the services of the leading 'heroic' novelist of the day to add 'colour.' They approached Jeffery Farnol through his agents; it was agreed that he should receive a return first-class passage to New York, all accommodation expenses, plus a fee of £500 for five short preliminary articles plus a 3-4000 word article on the fight itself, exclusive to the 'Mail.' The fight description later appeared in "Epics of The Fancy", published in 1928. The colour articles appeared in the 'Daily Mail' on June 25, 27, 28, 30, July 1 ,and July 2.

The fight took place in New Jersey on July 3, 1921, and Farnol's account appeared in the 'Daily Mail' on the following morning, July 4. Given the time difference of five hours, that meant that he had to write his description—all in longhand—and have it ready for transmission by around 10.30 in the evening, a matter of less than six hours after the end of the fight. Yet the account reads as though he had rewritten and polished it for a week or more; it is a tribute to Jeffery Farnol's mastery of the language.

Saturday June 25, 1921

CARPENTIER

Mr Jeffery Farnol visits his training quarters

From Jeffery Farnol, who has gone to New York as Special Correspondent to describe for readers of The Daily Mail *the fight for the heavy-weight boxing championship of the world, which takes place next Saturday. Below is a brief note on his first visit to Carpentier's training camp.*

Guided by Mr W.F. Bullock, the chief correspondent of *The Daily Mail* in the United States, I found my way to-day to the training quarters of Georges Carpentier at Manhasset, Long Island. I beheld him the same slender young athlete as of yore—in the hey-day of health and strength and full of that god-like confidence in himself which is surely the attribute of youth. I watched those long white, full-muscled arms flash as he smote the flickering punching ball and was unfeignedly thankful I was not in its place. I watched him pound his sparring partners round the ring, marking the quick light footwork of him, and the elusiveness of that light shapely body—a joy to behold—his punishing "infighting" and clean breakaways.

Descamps' joyous eye

But once or twice I thought him a little slower than usual and he seemed something short-winded. And once or twice (because I am only a Romancist) I glanced from these swift moving figures in the ring to the faces of one or two who watched (even as I). Many of these knew more of this great game than I by reason of longer experience, and on their faces I beheld a look that seemed to tell me that my own judgement was not at fault.

But the eye of M. Descamps, Carpentier's manager was bright and joyous and on his mobile lips was an enigmatic smile. I wondered if here was not some diplomatic understanding between him and his Georges—remembering that at this late period of his training Carpentier is the cynosure of eyes friendly and antagonistic.

Monday June 27, 1921

"GEORGES"
from Jeffery Farnol

In this city of lights and heights, that has grown out of all recognition since last I saw it twelve years ago, both as regards mileage, magnificence, and noise, I am struck with the broad divergence of opinion concerning the forthcoming fight between Dempsey and Carpentier for the championship of the world.

In the glittering halls of opulence, where flowers bloom, birds carol, and fountains play, where one may dine on the fat of the land, moistened occasionally by strange fruity decoctions, prettily pink and as expensive as they are sweet, the word seems to be "Carpentier!"

In vast salons, marble-pillared, cunningly-lighted, where footsteps are decorously hushed by carpets of velvet pile, where one may luxuriate in wonderfully easy chairs and a bottled mystery called "Near-Beer", one may catch, wafted to one's ears in feminine tones from palm-shaded corners, the name "Georges". Even those tip-chasing autocrats, the page-boys seem to follow the fashion more or less.

But the policeman on the corner, loose-coated, cap cocked over one cynical eye, chewing thoughtfully and swinging his bludgeon in weary boredom; how vastly different his opinion! Venture to question him, and he will suspend mastication awhile to view you slowly and speak something in this wise:

"Carponteer, j'er say? Gee! What's bitin' ye? Jack Dempsey'll eat him. Fast, d'ye say? What, Carponteer? Well, he's gotta be, I guess, and then some. Jack's gotta sleep pill in each mitt. Quick? Well, say: Jack's a live wire, Jack's a cyclone. Carponteer, huh!"

Whereafter our policeman will turn and go on masticating and club twirling like the ruler of men he is.

Let us slip quietly into one of those shops called "Delicatessen", where, among other comestibles, are to be had every variety of pickle under the sun and a beverage labelled "Grape Smack". Amid these luxuries let us question their vendor on the topic of the hour. He will answer: "De liddle Vrenchman no good! Jack Dempsey kill him quick. So! " Here a plump and greasy fist smites a greasy, plump palm and a plump and greasy head nods in quick asseveration. Thus New York is more or less a divided camp with its eyes turned expectantly towards those other two camps where the champions train and fit themselves to prove to this great city and the greater world beyond which of the twain is the better man.

Tuesday June 28, 1921

DEMPSEY'S BIG SLAP.
Fond of books, dogs, and children.

Mr Jeffery Farnol, who has gone to the United States to describe the fight for The Daily Mail *has had actual experience of boxing as an amateur. He has dealt largely with boxing in his popular novels* "The Amateur Gentleman" *and* "The Broad Highway".

Today I talked with the champion, whose often-pictured face is, I suppose, more or less familiar to the world in general. Therefore I will try briefly to describe the inner self no camera can portray and tell of Dempsey as I saw him.

I confess that with the majority of the uninitiated I held the belief that he was one with no thought beyond hard knocks and Carpentier.

Surely never were two combatants so utterly dissimilar in themselves, styles, or surroundings. Carpentier's camp is a lonely farmhouse, far remote, hidden amid orchards where no strange foot may intrude.

Dempsey's quarters here by the sea have no mystery, no locked doors; they are thronged daily by eager spectators. On his staff are many who bear famous names. Among these are Battling Nelson, an old acquaintance; Jack O'Brien, who recognised a friend in Harry Preston and immediately challenged him to three rounds, which, I believe will take place in Madison-square anon.

Speaking of the champion, merely as observer, I found no fighting animal but a genial young giant, full of health and the confidence it inspires; a man, besides, who is no dullard; a man who takes an intelligent interest in books. What is perhaps better, he has a soft corner in his heart for dogs and children.

Afterwards, watching him work in the ring, a grim, shapely figure, quick to adapt his style of defence to various sparring partners, noting the strength and speed of the feints and shifts of the head and light-treading feet, I wondered if any man could long endure the terrible might of him.

Thursday June 30, 1921

"SURE SOME FIGHT"
Views of the man with the oft-broken nose

from JEFFERY FARNOL *who has gone to the United States to describe the fight for* The Daily Mail *has had actual experience of boxing as an amateur. He has dealt largely with boxing in his popular novels "The Amateur Gentleman" and "The Broad Highway".*

The man with the oft-broken nose whose famous name was once trumpeted throughout the sporting world glanced at me beneath a craggy prominence of brow and nodded.

"Say, Jeff, " quoth he, "if you're writin' dope for fight fans, get next to this. It ain't no good pulling the highbrow stuff. Give it 'em straight and unwatered. And, say, you pen and ink guys ain't got no cushy job neither, seeing you can't dope out how Jack's going to behave on the day, any more than Jack himself can.

"Jack's fit 'n' strong, as you jest seen, and never better, but, then, so's George, and both sure of themselves, so what I tell you about their chances is to be took in small doses, good and cautious.

"I've been in the game all my life, and what I say is: No man knows how he's going to feel and act until he gets into the ring. Here's Jack with a knock-out in each hand, a man as has had more hard things said about him than any other guy in the United States, and took it all smiling. But say, friend, he ain't going to smile when he faces George Carpentier on Saturday—not so as you could notice it, he ain't; and if he connects with George's block, George'll sure know.

"No, sir; if Jack removes George's block altogether I ain't going to swoon away with amazement. On the other hand, there's George (with his pretty face and right mitt good for more than blowing kisses) out for all he can get for himself and the honour of France, with both eyes on the championship, an' doin' the mystery act along there at Manhasset, mighty sure that the only guy on two legs that can flatten out Jack for keeps is George Carpentier; which if he does, ain't going to make me swallow down no flies gasping in amazement, as you book writers say.

"Only, the man as wins on Saturday is sure going to be some fighter. And that's that."

"But you haven't told me very much," said I.

"Jeff," quoth my hero of a hundred fights, shaking his battered head at me. "I ain't no spiritualist, nor yet one as dopes out the future from piping off crystals and that kind of slush. I'm only one as has been there, and all I can tell you or anybody else is what everybody else will know on Saturday. Anyway, except a lucky blow is landed early it will sure be some fight. One thing is sure—one of 'em will win!"

In Dempsey's camp I met many other veterans of the game; genial souls, for the most part, clear-eyed, quick-moving men, looking fit and able, from whom I gleaned one outstanding and universal belief—namely, that unless Carpentier can win early in the fight Dempsey's capacity for endurance and punishment will give him the victory.

Friday July 1, 1921

NEW YORK'S ONE TOPIC
Men and women agog with the fight

from JEFFERY FARNOL who has gone to the United States to describe the fight for The Daily Mail *has had actual experience of boxing as an amateur. He has dealt largely with boxing in his popular novels* "The Amateur Gentleman" *and* "The Broad Highway".

As the day of the great fight approaches public interest and excitement grow apace. "The Fight" is the chief topic of conversation among high and low. In club and drawing room, on street corners, in factories and stores, men and women argue pro and con regarding the chances of the two combatants, and, espousing the cause of one or the other, wax warm and enthusiastic.

And herein I find matter for no small wonder since these zealous partisans, or at least the vast majority, never saw a prize fight in their lives and have no intention of witnessing this one. And yet, perhaps, this is no such great cause for surprise after all, because we humans—and women more especially, dearly love a conflict, since by strife, either mental or physical, character is developed.

In my peregrinations to and fro, I have observed this to be more particularly marked in those of the gentle sex whose ages approximate 60 and 16. Sixty, who bears a coronet of silver hair regally and unashamed in this unageing age, pronounces herself for Carpentier because " he is so elegant" and has such an engaging smile in his pictures, and she is sure he is quite a nice young man. Sixteen or thereabouts, crossing silken limbs and flicking the ash from her cigarette, declares that "nothing will satisfy me but a clean knock-out."

The page that matters

As to the sterner sex? Behold this great club reading room where menials flit unheard and members lounge in padded chairs imbibing strange moistnesses from long glasses, and dab at perspiring brows by reason of hot weather and "this dry and thirsty land"; peep cautiously over their shoulders , and I will wager a fivespot (5 dollars) to a hayseed that nine times out of ten it is the sporting page that absorbs them.

What a wealth of metaphor, what a host of details, what meticulous descriptions are here! I have read whole columns of close print concerning Carpentier's right arm and as much again devoted to Dempsey's legs and torso. Here also one may read very much of shifts, hooks, jabs, swings, and stances, of blocks to be knocked off, of the tapping of spheres, shadow boxing and other mysterious technicalities.

What wonder that the weary businessman, perspiring despite his straw hat and Shantung suit, wrestles desperately with his evening journal in crowded car that he may read the latest about such wonders.

Thus stimulated by newspapers, by murmurs of dissension in one camp or the other, by dreadful apprehensions that after all the fight may be forbidden by those loathed and mysterious tyrants "the authorities", excitement soars hourly. I, whose easier part it is to watch, wonder within myself if the two men chiefly concerned feel anything of nerve-strain because of this, and, despite all their reported fitness and confidence in themselves to knock each other's "block" off, have any glimmering conception of the world's trepidation; and I am sincerely thankful that instead of being Georges Carpentier or Jack Dempsey, champion of the world, I am only Jeffery Farnol.

Saturday July 2, 1921

RAIN IN NEW YORK.
Carpentier's supporters on his generalship.

from JEFFERY FARNOL who has gone to the United States to describe the fight for The Daily Mail *has had actual experience of boxing as an amateur. He has dealt largely with boxing in his popular novels "The Amateur Gentleman" and "The Broad Highway".*

In a few short hours it is estimated that some 100,000 reasoning beings, braving the difficulties of travel and discomfort in crowded conveyances, and with nothing to allay the pangs of hunger but such scanty provisions as they can bear about their persons, will gather themselves into one circumscribed space beneath the July sun to watch two men pound each other about an 18-foot ring.

It is still raining. The weather man's forecast for to-day was "fair", and fair has meant a distinctly cool, damp morning with an overcast sky and intermittent drizzle. The forecast for tomorrow is "fair", and tens of thousands of eyes, many of which have travelled several thousands of miles to look upon tomorrow's epic battle, are this morning gazing with almost painful intensity up to the wet, grey clouds which cover the city without a break.

The feeling of tenseness which has existed in the air of New York since the first day of this great week grows hourly. In trains and "tubes" this morning men and women could be heard discussing the events of tomorrow in short, staccato sentences which people unconsciously adopt who are labouring under great excitement. The talk shifts from the arena to Manhasset, from there to Atlantic City.

Strain of last hours.

Most people's thoughts seem to dwell more than anything on the two contestants waiting in their respective camps for the hour to strike. They seem by a sort of sympathy to feel the intense agony of suspense which they imagine the fighters must be undergoing. As all the work of training is over they have nothing to do but sit about and think. It seems incredible that the last night won't be a nerve-wracking experience for both men, but so far at least they are to all appearances the least worried persons for a hundred miles around.

Dempsey spent the greater part of yesterday reclining in a porch receiving friends and dispensing jokes. If he had just won the fight he could not have been more cheerful.

I paid my last visit to Carpentier's camp early to-day and found everyone there, too, in the highest spirits. Descamps (Carpentier's manager) said: "Ah, my Georges never fooled me yet. After tomorrow, I will be the manager of the world's heavyweight champion." Carpentier's trainer, Gus Wilson, said: "Georges knows too much for Dempsey." Captain J.H.Mallet, the challenger's friend and adviser, said: "Georges has always risen to the occasion. He has never yet failed to carry out his intentions and he intends to beat Dempsey."

Lieutenant Pierre Mallet, the challenger's war comrade: "We believe Carpentier's experience and ring generalship will carry him through to victory."

Joe Jeannette: "Carpentier is too smart a fighter to lose this bout. He will be away when Dempsey hits and the champion will not be able to see his right hand, it will be that fast."

Charles Ledoux: "Georges knows how to take care of himself."

Marcel Denys, the French light-weight: "Georges will win with a one-two punch and I don't think Dempsey will be able to hit him one telling blow."

Joe Gans, sparring partner: "I believe Carpentier will knock out Dempsey in the fourth or fifth round with a right to the jaw."

Chris Arnold, sparring partner: "Carpentier has a right hand that never misses and it paralyses when it strikes."

Carpentier's brain work.

The most interesting comments of all came from William A. Brady, manager successively to James J. Corbett and James Jeffries. He said: "When Jack Dempsey faces Georges Carpentier in the ring at Jersey City he will meet the fastest, brainiest, trickiest, hardest-hitting boxer he has ever encountered. Carpentier will prove a 'fifteen' puzzle to Dempsey, who will find no slow-moving, slow-thinking Fulton, Willard or Morris before him.

"He will meet a pastmaster, as brave as they make them, with a punch that, if it reaches the spot, will render Dempsey or any other fighter in the world *hors de combat*. I am not underrating Dempsey. He is a wonderful specimen, but I saw him box Brennan. If that contest was an honest one, and I think it was, then it should be evens on tomorrow's match.

"Carpentier is a far better man than Brennan, and if he hits Dempsey as easily as Brennan did it will be all over but shouting. I am a great believer in psychology before the men meet in the ring and the gong sounds.

"When the articles were signed at my office Carpentier and Dempsey met for the first time. Kearns (Dempsey's manager) proposed that he should sign for Dempsey, but Carpentier insisted on Dempsey signing personally. We waited two hours for Dempsey's arrival. It was plain to me that the Frenchman planned to have a good look at his prospective opponent before sailing back to France. Dempsey arrived. Carpentier, like a shot, sprang to his feet, crossed to Dempsey, and, while he carelessly felt Dempsey's muscles, slapped his thighs, and felt his calves, gave him a complete looking over.

Golf together.

Laughing, he filled the air with admiring shouts. "Magnifique, tremendous, superb, wonderful, Monsieur Jacques." Meantime Dempsey stood speechless at the superb impudence of the other man, and, in fact, did not open his mouth for five minutes after. Dempsey remembers that.

"Next day they played 18 holes at golf together. It seemed queer to fight followers, but I am told you can study a man very well on the golf course. I wonder if that is why the wily Descamps arranged that golf game.

"It will be an interesting study to watch the demeanour of the two men between the ring entrance and the sound of the gong. It may tell the story of the fight in advance. I am not predicting that Dempsey will lose his title, but I am willing for it to go on record that he faces the fight of his life tomorrow.

"My opinion is that the bout will end in a knock-out before the end of the sixth round, and if it comes in one of the earlier rounds Carpentier will be the victor. If it becomes a question of endurance and ability to take a beating Dempsey will win."

Monday July 4, 1921

Graphic account of the fight
THE AMERICAN'S STRENGTH.

Taking blows like a stone wall. Carpentier's drive to the jaw.

From JEFFERY FARNOL
This well-known English author, who began life as a boxer, was specially commissioned by The Daily Mail *to go to the United States for the purpose of describing the great fight between Dempsey, the champion of the world, and*

Carpentier, the champion of Europe. In the following cablegram, written immediately after the American boxer's victory, he gives a word-picture which, we think, will enable our readers to visualize very clearly one of the greatest scenes in the annals of the ring.

We arrived in good time at the place of combat, a huge circular wooden structure rising tier on tier, a very wilderness of seats, sparsely filled as yet.

Being ushered forthwith into my place, I had ample leisure to look round upon this vast amphitheatre that was to accommodate one hundred thousand spectators. And ever they came, a straw-hatted multitude from all quarters, pouring down the broad aisles, a cheery, genial multitude agog with expectation.

It was a close and sultry day, although the sky was dark with heavy clouds pierced here and there by a coppery glow. But beneath this lowering canopy all was stir and bustle—voices, laughter, shouted greetings, the tread of countless feet; an indescribable sound made up of many sounds and pierced ever and anon by the loud cries of those who vended sandwiches, ginger ale, and the ubiquitous peanut; while a band, blessedly remote, blared fitful music.

Moment by moment the throng increased, an unending procession, and always it seemed the day grew hotter, until the stifling discomfort was relieved by a few drops of rain accompanied by a breath of cool wind.

Sea of faces.
Tier upon tier to a lofty skyline.

There had been rumours of trouble owing to forged tickets, but never have I seen a more orderly, better-tempered crowd, nor one so vast. Nor could these perspiring thousands have been handled better even by our own police.

Still, one was necessarily subjected to some discomfort; myself particularly so, on account of such as came later than I; these being for the most part very large plethoric men, short of wind and shorter of manners, who thrust themselves past and over me at unpleasantly frequent intervals.

However, these having jostled themselves into their places and being securely wedged while they regale upon divers viands and suck strange fluids out of bottles by means of straws, I take occasion to stand upon my chair and look about me. And here is a sight to be remembered, for the huge amphi-theatre is filled at last, or nearly so.

Faces! a dense, ever-stirring mass, pinkly nebulous; a sea of faces, spreading from the ringside up and up, tier on tier, to the lofty skyline; a troubled sea, rippling with constant motion and murmurous with vague clamour.

I stood awed by this stupendous spectacle.

Suddenly the clamour subsided as into the ring stepped the Announcer, furnished with a megaphone, which—either through excitement or lack of knowledge—he managed so ill that his naturally hoarse voice sounded hoarser and more muffled than Nature had made it.

Preliminary competitors were introduced, and bout followed bout to the accompaniment of shouts and cheers, though it was evident that the great concourse was impatient for the star turn and eager for the moment when the two proved champions should face each other.

Roar of cheers

So the multitude watched and cheered and sweltered in the heat, while aeroplanes swooped, circled, and buzzed overhead, and the preliminary bouts were fought through. Then shouts and uproar died away as forth stood the Announcer, faithfully clutching the mouthpiece of his megaphone, and began forthwith to bellow more muffled incoherencies.

He paused suddenly to point with extended arm, when up rose a murmur that swelled to a shout—a very roar of welcome—as into the fateful ring, surrounded by his backers and satellites, stepped Georges Carpentier. Truly a proud moment this for any man, to behold this tempest of waving straw hats flourished in his honour, to hear his name roared by a hundred thousand throats; and I watched Carpentier as he stood wrapped in his dressing-gown bowing to the universal acclaim, his face as pale and serene, his smile as placidly assured, as it had been in the quiet of the Manhasset farmhouse.

Scarcely had he taken his corner when Dempsey appeared, looming bigger and bulkier even than when he had shaken my hand at his training quarters and told me he was fond of books. His appearance was greeted by cheers, it is true, but nothing like the wild ovation accorded to his rival.

Hardly was he seated when Descamps appeared at his elbow full of smiles and chatty, yet very quiet and keen to watch each fold of the tape about Dempsey's powerful fists.

I remarked how the two antagonists smiled and gripped each other's hands; with what a kindly, assured air Carpentier patted the champion's mighty shoulder.

And now I, in common with all other ordinary beings, fell to a state of nerve-racking tension; a sweating, short-breathing, sighful suspense.

A man laughed high and shrill, somebody whistled, but for the most part it was a dull, uneasy, murmuring period. With due care and deliberation the gloves were drawn on and secured, seconds and satellites vanished from the ring, and there fell a silence, a strange stillness, a hush of breathless expectancy wherein the eyes of some 90,000 spectators focussed themselves upon these two men.

And now it seemed to me that Dempsey, with his great bulk and height, had much the semblance of a lion; while Carpentier, all slender grace, possessed the lithe supple-ness of a panther.

Then the bell clanged. The two sprang together, and the stamp of their feet woke pandemonium, for the FIRST ROUND of the great fight had begun.

I saw Carpentier's glove flash twice in rapid succession to Dempsey's jaw; but this lion-like man, apparently quite unshaken, staggered his lighter antagonist with a counter to the body. Carpentier, having landed these two smashing blows that should have felled any ordinary man, kept away, seeming to realise the futility of such methods, and verily it looked to me much like playing a tattoo on a stone wall.

Georges' nose split.
Desperate courage against great odds.

All about me was a hoarse, roaring clamour that rose to frenzy at each telling blow, for now the fighting was fast and furious. Round and round they circled, these champions of the game, feinting and dodging with twinkling feet and whirling arms, Carpentier countering Dempsey's terrible drives with stiff upper-cuts and swings to the head. Then they fell to a clinch, and, watching Dempsey's fists at work, it seemed to me that Carpentier could have small chance against such terribly punishing infighting; for the champion's gloves seemed everywhere, now battering his ribs, now thudding on the jaw or under the chin, until Carpentier's long, lithe body rocked and swayed and I heard myself calling to him "Keep away!" though my voice was quite lost in the universal din.

Suddenly they broke free, and I saw Carpentier bruised and battered, his nose split, his face spattered with blood. Stooping, he swung a right to Dempsey's head, and there ensued a flurry of hard-smitten blows; but whereas Dempsey seemed strong as ever, Carpentier was evidently weakened.

Fighting desperately, he was forced to the ropes, and there tried to cover up against the fury of Dempsey's attack, and, finding this vain, clinched.

As they were parted he slipped and fell across the second rope of the ring, whereupon his opponent promptly stepped back, and Carpentier, springing to his feet, was fighting with desperate courage as the gong sounded.

And thus ended ROUND ONE, much in Dempsey's favour; and I saw the truth of the saying that a clever little one, howsoever courageous, may never conquer a clever big man who is equally courageous.

I sat staring at Dempsey's broad back glistening with water from the sponge; I heard people shouting to one another; I was aware of others questioning me, but I paid scant heed, being amazed that a man so big and strong as Dempsey could be so amazingly quick, and wondering how long Carpentier could possibly last, this same graceful, gentle-mannered Carpentier, who had been so sublimely confident in himself and his destiny—and then the bell clanged for the SECOND ROUND.

Dempsey advanced crouching low, his stooped head swaying, his left shoulder drawn up to protect his jaw from Carpentier's avenging right. Thus he dodged his opponent round the ring, wary and watchful for an opening, but Carpentier was as cautious.

Carpentier retreated, poised on his toes, his left arm extended and his right hand drawn back ready to strike. Suddenly, in he sprang, with a stabbing left to the chin and a heavy right to the head; but Dempsey scarcely heeded, and followed steadily in relentless pursuit.

Again Carpentier flashed in with a left hook and was out again, exhibiting such footwork as was a joy to behold, and once again the air rang with an ecstatic hubbub.

For a while Carpentier kept away—and small wonder, for that smashing blow had injured his wrist and broken his thumb, though this was not known until long after the fight was ended.

Followed a clinch wherein the champion, once again proved he was Carpentier's master at in-fighting, pounding him severely before the referee ordered them to "break away!" And now, beholding Carpentier bruised and bleeding, his comely features so woefully marred, I grieved for him; my pity changing to loud-voiced joy as, with another pantherine leap, he smote the iron Dempsey between the eyes and, ducking the return, swung right and left to the champion's body; and so, lightly away and out of danger; and I was cheering again like any maniac.

Carpentier's round.

And now it was that Dempsey, following his agile opponent with the same dogged determination, seemed for a wonder a little shaken and confused and lowered his guard for a moment, whereupon Carpentier was upon him with whirling blows, jabs, and hooks and a flush right-handed punch that shook even this lion-like Dempsey at last and sent him staggering back to the ropes.

Once again pandemonium reigned, the great amphitheatre roared and raved with such tumultuous clamour as might almost have been heard in New York City, or, at least, so I thought, for indeed there was scarce a man in all the surrounding multitude who did not realise that here was a dramatic climax.

Carpentier saw it too, and quick as ever, despite the punishment he had endured, drove a clean and powerful right. to the champion's jaw that shook him from head to foot, so that he leaned there against the ropes, his arms hanging, dizzy with blows and open to Carpentier's attack.

The sight of him standing thus, swaying a little and seemingly helpless against his smaller antagonist, wrought the raving spectators to a very frenzy. In Carpentier's corner that excitable, fiery little man, M. Descamps, was more so than ever, but his voice was drowned by 90,000 other voices, for now, if ever, was Carpentier's opportunity.

But great boxers, like ordinary human beings, are prone to such weaknesses as over-anxiety, flurry, and their attendant disadvantages. Carpentier went in to win, smote with his left and missed, struck with his right and missed. Then, before he could try again, Dempsey slid into a clinch and battered his opponent's ribs.

Carpentier broke clear, danced to the right, skipped to the left, and smashed home a blow to the champion's face that rocked him on his heels.

Once again Carpentier smote, but Dempsey, recovering somewhat, blocked the punch and clinched again, only to meet Carpentier's fist in a lightning upper-cut. Time and again Carpentier staggered him so that I marvelled at his uncanny strength and endurance, for, though slow now and heavy-footed, he took these blows and still came for more.

But Carpentier, either because of weariness, or his hurts, or over-anxiety, or, most probably, because of all these, was short in his distance time and again, and missed many opportunities.

Dempsey's recovery.

I thought, too, that Dempsey's senses began to clear. Up came his great left shoulder protecting that salient feature, his jaw, and once again he began to carry the fight to Carpentier, cutting him between the eyes just as the gong ended round two. And this, as was plain to see, was greatly in favour of Carpentier

Dempsey rose with the sound of the bell for the THIRD ROUND, and advanced swiftly but with new caution, his face well protected. Suddenly he drove fiercely with his right, but the blow was wild, and, gracefully ducking it, Carpentier swung right and left to the jaw and dodged out of range. Hereupon the champion came on, following his opponent with the grim determination that was characteristic of him, but he seemed slow and heavy in contrast to Carpentier's swift elusiveness and wonderful footwork as, dodging out of a clinch, the Frenchman swung repeatedly with left and right, but seemed a little short.

Always Dempsey came on, chin drawn low, mighty shoulders bowed, fists ready to strike; fists, these, either of which could end the fight did they but reach their mark. Wherefor the crowd rocked and swayed and yelled. And I gazed, moist by reason of the hot day and a growing anxiety for the lesser man.

Repeatedly Carpentier's blows got home, but always too lightly, and as often he eluded those deadly clinches; but, despite his blows and his quickness of foot, Dempsey got to him at last, and they were breast to breast.

Noting Carpentier's worn face as he strove to block that terrible infighting, my anxiety for him grew. Even as I watched I saw the champion's fists shake him with repeated upper-cuts on his bleeding face. But as they drew apart Carpentier sprang in again with a hard-driven right that stopped the champion's relentless advance a while and hope revived.

Then, as suddenly, Carpentier staggered wild-eyed, and no one, unless it were himself, was more glad to hear the bell than I.

And thus ended round three, to Dempsey's advantage, though on this head there was some discussion among spectators in my neighbourhood.

Promptly Carpentier rose for the FOURTH ROUND, his left eye and cheek much swollen. This time it was evident he meant to keep out of range until he could find an opening for that right hand of his, which had shaken even the mighty Dempsey in the second round. It was plain that Carpentier was weary and weak, and small wonder, remembering the pace they had fought the three preceding rounds. Once Carpentier reached his adversary's face, but the blow lacked strength, and in return he took a hard jab to the body ere he clinched, only to receive more punishment on the ribs and face.

When they broke away Carpentier seemed still weaker, yet ever and anon, with some recovery of his old lightning quickness, he shook Dempsey with a right and left. To and fro they fought, now at long range, now smiting viciously in clinches, but as I watched the gallant Frenchman it seemed more than ever clear that he strove against hopeless odds, and I turned to view the tense faces of my neighbours, some of whom waved their arms and began to shout deliriously, " He's got it!" "Attaboy! He's finished!" And, looking whither they all looked, I saw Carpentier's white body sagged and crumpled, saw him drop upon his hands and knees and sink face down upon the canvas floor.

The roar and hubbub about me grew faint and far away, for all my senses were focussed upon the rise and fall of the referee's arm where he bent above the prostrate figure. Slowly, slowly, the limp form gathered itself together and the brave Frenchman rose, glancing about him a little vaguely and with an effort at the old serene smile that I thought very pitiful to see. And now it was Dempsey's turn, and in he went determined to end the fight once and for all.

Blocking Carpentier's lead, he drove a flush hit to the face. Carpentier tried vainly to cover up against the rain of blows that beset him, staggered suddenly, and, throwing out wild arms, fell heavily and lay outstretched and forlorn while the referee again began the count.

Once, prompted by the indomitable soul of him, he strove to rise. His arms moved, his legs jerked spasmodically, but the poor flesh, unequal to the call of the unconquerable spirit, did but writhe, pitifully helpless, and the great fight was over.

Carpentier's mistake.

The Lion had beaten the Panther; the big clever man had conquered the small clever man, and Champion Jack Dempsey is champion still.

And now, with fresh laurels on his somewhat battered brow, the champion turned to meet the adulation of the multitude. The ring was thronged with those eager to congratulate him, but I (standing upon my chair and none now to pull me down or remonstrate, since all did the same), perched thus, I strove vainly to catch some glimpse of the fallen man, nor did I relax my effort until at last I beheld him on his feet, though still groggy, doing his best to smile and be congratulated by his conqueror, which is one of the rules of the game.

And presently the great crowds began to melt and vanish as do all crowds, soon or late. And I, being seated once more, consulted my watch, only to find that this great fight which had drawn hither so vast a number of people, many of whom had travelled far across seas and continents, had lasted exactly ten minutes and a few odd seconds.

Thus have I tried to picture this wonderful scene, one I shall never forget, and tried to describe this fight as truly and faithfully as I may. If any should wonder why Carpentier lasted no longer than the fourth round I would say that in my humble opinion his mistake was in the first round when, instead of following his usual tactics of "hit and away," he closed with a man who is his master at in-fighting. Had he, on the contrary, boxed at long range, trusting to his incomparable quickness and footwork, his judgment of time and pace, there might have been a different tale to tell.

Jeffery Farnol's first story accepted for publication, around 1895/6 was called 'Jones, A.B.' He continued writing short stories as well as working on his novels, and, during his eight years in New York, would haunt the offices of the leading magazines between his scene-painting chores. This story, 'Rejecting Philomela', was originally titled 'A Case of Friendship', and was most probably written around 1908; by a letter dated July 11, 1911, Edward Farnol submitted it to Farnol's agents, A.P.Watt & Sons, together with two other short stories. They were successful in placing it with 'Good Housekeeping' (U.S.) for the March, 1912 edition. Although the action supposedly takes place in New England, the story is very British in tone and atmosphere. It was accompanied in 'Good Housekeeping' by a full page illustration by Henry Hutt.

REJECTING PHILOMELA

The Romance of a Young Man Who Refused to Get Married

EDITOR'S NOTE—*If your stern but loving parent insisted on selecting your life-mate, how would you meet the vexing situation? The brilliant author of this story furnishes a novel and highly enjoyable solution.*

I found Bagshorne in his den. He was sitting, or rather lying, in a deep saddle-bag chair, with his slippered feet among the litter of books ,and papers upon the table, and the air was heavy with smoke from the short-stemmed, big-bowled briar between his teeth, which somehow seemed a part of himself.

I dragged up another chair, and, sitting down, plunged into my subject at once.

"Bagshorne," I began, "what's a fellow to do when his governor insists on his marrying?"

"Why, marry, of course," replied Bagshorne, between the puffs at his pipe.

"Wait!" I said. "'Supposing a fellow's governor fixes everything before hand, without so much as a 'by your leave'; supposing the fellow happens to know that the lady in question is eccentric and all that—how then?"

"Why, then, don't marry," said. Bagshorne.

"Certainly, but the question is how to avoid it," I pursued. " You know what a confounded—er—'Roman parent', my governor is."

"Perhaps, after all, you'd better marry, you know," he nodded; "What's she like, though?"

"My dear chap," I answered, "that's the ridiculous part of the affair. I've never so much as seen her."

"Name then?" he inquired, laconically.

"Esther Clarges."

Bagshorne removed his pipe with a jerk, stared thoughtfully up at the ceiling, and chuckled.

"Ho!" he exclaimed. "And eccentric you say?"

"Yes, won't live in town, you know. Has a farm in one of the New England states and keeps pigs and things."

Bagshorne knocked the ashes from his pipe and chuckled again. Bagshorne has a most irritating chuckle.

"The situation seems to amuse you," I said indignantly. "I can quite understand its appearing highly humorous to such a nature as yours, but to one possessing any of the finer feelings, it would appeal as one of life's tragedies—hopes, dreams, ideals, all shattered!"

"Got a match?" inquired Bagshorne. There is a callous brutality about my friend Bagshorne at times which I can only explain by the fact that he was an editor at one period of his career, from the effects of which he has never quite recovered. He relighted his pipe, and puffed thoughtfully for a moment or so.

"Question is," he said suddenly, "will she accept you?"

"We can't be certain of that," I answered, "but there's always the confounded risk you know. The fact is," I continued, "it seems as if the best thing I could do would be to write and—er—put her off, so to speak."

Bagshorne shook his head. "Shouldn't do that."

"Why not?"

"Oh, well, I shouldn't."

"Nonsense, Bagshorne," I exclaimed, "under such ridiculous circumstances, it's the only course left open to me. I shall write here and now, and expect you to give me your assistance."

"Certainly," nodded Bagshorne, as I rummaged out pens and paper. "Certainly. How would this do?":

Dear Madam:

We much regret that, owing to lack of space, we are unwillingly compelled—

"I'm in no joking humor, Bagshorne," I broke in; "I'm dead serious."

"Great mistake," said Bagshorne with a tobacco-ey sigh. "In affairs of this kind, seriousness never pays."

Forthwith I drew up to the table and there was silence for a while, broken only by the scratching of my pen and the wheeze of Bagshorne's pipe.

"Finished?" he inquired, as I paused.

"No, merely stuck for an idea. I'll read you what I've got; you may be able to suggest something:

"Dear Miss Clarges:
"Your guardian and my respected father have been getting their heads together, with the result that they are determined to bring about a marriage between us, as you are probably aware by this time.
"Judging from my own feelings in the matter, I do not doubt that the idea is anything but pleasing to you. That I should not love you is scarcely to he wondered at, considering that I have never seen you, and the statement therefore can neither pain nor surprise you.

"I will freely confess that mine is a nature to which the idea of marriage, even in the vaguest, most abstract form, is wholly abhorrent. I feel that I am morally unfitted for the state."

"Humph!" said Bagshorne, as I ended, "what's it all mean—that 'vaguest, most abstract form' part, eh?"

"To tell you the truth I don't exactly know," I returned; "but it looks all right, and she can read her own meaning into it—that's the best of it."

Bagshorne shook his head.

"I could have done it much better, more effectively, and with a lot fewer words," he grumbled.

"How?"

"First"—he began ticking off each item upon his thumb with his pipe-stem—"you might suggest that you are habitually intoxicated; second, that you are devoted to tobacco, principally chewing, and third—yes, third, you might take snuff. There you have it," he said with a complacent wave of the hand; "concise and to the point. I could write it up into a very telling paragraph. I fancy it would damp the ardor of any girl, but if you think there's any doubt about it, you might run in something about—"

"I'll be hanged if I do," I broke in. "I'll perjure myself for no one. Besides, she'd take me for some brutalized savage."

"Exactly," said Bagshorne, gazing up at the slow-mounting smoke wreaths with a dreamy eye. "Of course she would."

"Well, I won't perjure myself for anyone," I repeated.

"Have it your own way, my dear chap," he sighed, writhing himself into a more comfortable position among the cushions. "It's your affair, not mine, only—"

"Well?", I inquired as he paused to emit a vast cloud of smoke.

"Only, I should certainly advise you to chew!"

"I shall confine myself purely to facts," I answered decisively.

"That's a pity," he said as I took up my pen, and there followed another interval of silence.

"Well?" he inquired at last, as I leaned back in my chair with a sigh. "Well?"

"I fancy so," I nodded. "What do *you* think?" And commencing from where I had previously left off, I read as follows:

"You have, I believe met my respected father, and must have observed that he is—shall I say, a man of strong character, very objectionably so, and will undoubtedly bring about a meeting between us sooner or later. Now the only escape I can see from this very awkward situation, my dear Miss Clarges, is for you to refuse the offer I shall, seeing the very objectionable strength of my 'Roman parent's' character,—be forced to make to you—that you will refuse me firmly and decisively, so that I may truthfully subscribe myself,

"Yours very obliged,
"RICHARD HUNTING.

"What do you think of it?" I inquired with a certain complacency, as I addressed the envelope. "All right, isn't it?"

"It's very beautiful," returned Bagshorne, "but you won't send it, of course."

"I most certainly shall."

"Oh, very good," said he. "Have a cigar." And he pursued, after a moment's reflection, "What do you say to a week's tramp into the country together?"

"Done!" I answered.

Goddesses In Disguise

"Seems rather a nice place," said Bagshorne on a certain afternoon a few days later, and he pointed to where the chimneys of a rambling farmhouse peeped at us above the motionless tops. It was a hot, still afternoon, yet the very stillness seemed full of the hum and drone of insects, broken now and then by the distant bark of a dog, or the drowsy lowing of cows standing knee deep in a pool beneath the shade of a row of elms.

Bagshorne made the unnecessary remark that it was warm, and sinking upon the grass began to fill his pipe

"That would make a fine sketch," I said, taking out my book, "and I haven't drawn a line since we started."

Bagshorne lay beside me, with an occasional groan of enjoyment over his pipe, watching me with lazy interest.

"If you were to give up wasting your time writing impossible stories, and stick to your drawing, you might manage to keep yourself some day," he volunteered.

"That's just where you're wrong, my chap," I returned; "that last story I sent you was a masterpiece in its way."

"Yes, but which way?" he inquired drowsily. "You see," I continued, ignoring his remark, "it required the mind of a poet to justly appreciate that story, and you are scarcely a poet, are you, Baggy?" He leaned back, tilting his hat over his nose, and appeared to think it over. Glancing toward him a few minutes later I saw that it had evidently been too much for him—he was asleep. I worked on steadily, until I became aware that evening was approaching, for already the meadows glowed a richer gold, and behind the elms the sun was setting in a glory of red flame.

"Bagshorne!" I ejaculated, "just look at that sun effect."

Bagshorne grunted from underneath his hat, and kicked one leg feebly.

"Bagshorne!"

"Hallo," he sighed.

"It's simply magnificent, my dear chap."

"What is?" he inquired, without stirring.

"The sunset!"

"Thanks!" he said in a besotted voice.

"By Jove!" I continued, "if I had only brought some colors with me! It looks from here as if those trees were wrapped in one seething flame."

"Let 'em seethe," moaned Bagshorne.

"It beats anything I ever saw before," I continued.

"Awfully jolly," he grunted, "grass nice and soft, too!"

"That remark," I said, glancing to where he wallowed beside me, "is entirely in keeping with your base, material nature, Bagshorne—you are singularly deficient in soul."

He was silent for a while gazing sleepily toward a row of red roofed barns.

"Hallo!" he exclaimed suddenly, "there's a girl," and following his glance I saw her. She was clad in a white dress of some thin material that showed every subtle curve in her shapely figure. Upon her head was a great blue sunbonnet, and two pails swung from an old-fashioned yoke upon her shoulders.

"What a superb figure," I exclaimed involuntarily. "By Jove! I'll ask her for a drink."But at this moment, catching sight of us, or more probably noting the abandoned posture of Bagshorne, she swerved, intending to pass us at a safer distance.

Now, as I say, I was extremely thirsty, and there was, besides, something mightily attractive about that sunbonnet, therefore I rose to my feet and stole after her. It was with a certain nameless pleasure that I noticed the supple ease with which she managed the heavy pails, and how wonderfully slender was the ankle that peeped at me beneath her skirts. Having lingered behind a sufficient time to note these things at my leisure, I hurried forward and accosted her with an old world bow and flourish of my hat.

"Your pardon, dear maid, but whither away so fast? Prithee, stay one moment." She turned swiftly, and I saw a face framed in rebellious red-gold hair which quite overflowed the big sunbonnet.

"Sir!" she said, and there was something in the tone of her voice and the proud carriage of her head so altogether unexpected that I stood foolishly staring while surprise, anger, and amusement struggled for mastery in the blue depths of her eyes.

"I—I beg your pardon," I stammered at length. "I'm afraid I have made a—a mistake—that is, I'm awfully thirsty and I thought perhaps you would be so good—"

She laughed, and I remember it struck me as very sweet and musical.

"Which means, I suppose, that you would like some milk?" she said.

"If you would be so good," I answered, fishing out my flask.

As she stooped above the pail, I caught a glimpse of a round white arm that set me marveling. Was it customary, I wondered, to find young goddesses disguised as milk-maids in this part of the world—and with such arms and ankles, too?

She handed me the milk with a little smiling curtsey which I returned with another deep bow ere raising the flask to my lips. As I did so our eyes met and so for a delightful moment we stood, and I noticed that her long thick lashes were of a darker shade than her hair, and as for her eyes—

"Hallo, Philomela!" said a voice at this moment, and, turning, we beheld Bagshorne. The spell was broken.

"Harold!" exclaimed the goddess.

"Even so," said Bagshorne, and, lifting his hat lazily, he stooped and, kissed her with the most matter-of-fact air in the world.

I positively gasped with surprise.

"Seems you've done without me. Too late to introduce you, I suppose?"

"No," I answered, feeling a burning desire to kick him severely, "fact is—er—"

"Exactly!" said Bagshorne. "Why, then, Cousin Philomela, let me introduce my friend, Richard Hunting." Philomela glanced at me with a sudden quick look, and I almost fancied her red lips quivered suspiciously.

"Now that's the worst of Bagshorne, Miss Philomela—he is so close! I had no idea until a moment ago that he had a cousin."

"Why, you never asked, you know," he said idiotically, "and that reminds me, we 're awfully hungry, Phil."

"I'm afraid dinner won't be ready for some time yet," she answered, as she led us through the orchard toward the dairy. "You see, you are earlier than the time you gave in your letter."

"That's Dick's fault," grumbled Bagshorne. "He's so confoundedly energetic."

"Letter!" I exclaimed. "But I never knew."

"Exactly," said Bagshorne, "of course not. How should you?"

I felt decidedly irritated at his calm assurance. "But"—I was beginning rather angrily, when Philomela gently interrupted me.

"Your rooms are quite ready," she said. "Mrs. Bagget and I saw to everything. Yours, Mr. Hunting, overlooks the farmyard, but you won't mind that, will you?"

"Delighted!" I said, "only I wish I had come a little better prepared."

"Oh, we are quite unconventional here." she laughed, spreading out the skirt of her print gown.

"Besides," interpolated Bagshorne, "you've got your toothbrush."

"Oh, Harold," laughed Philomela, "it's my turn now. I have a surprise for *you*—Betty Carlyon is here."

"Good Lord!" exclaimed Bagshorne, and set down the pails with a bang. "And I haven't brought a solitary collar!"

"But you've got an extra pair of boots in the knapsack," I said, with a very fair imitation of his chuckle.

"So glad of that," laughed a voice behind us, and turning I was, next moment, making my bow to Miss Carlyon. She was dressed in the same way as her friend, only this time the sunbonnet was pink, and the handsome face beneath it was rendered more bewitching by the thick black braid of hair that hung down on either shoulder.

As she and Bagshorne led the way into the great stone-flagged kitchen, Philomela turned to me with a mischievous smile: "They are awfully fond of each other, you know, but they are always quarreling. The last time was six months ago, and they have not seen each other since."

"Bagshorne in love is something new," I laughed, "but then, he is nothing if not surprising."

What Happened Early in the Morning

It is an extraordinary thing that if a man chances to find himself in perfect harmony with life at any period of his existence, that period is one that seems to slip away faster than any other. Thus I woke up to the fact one morning that nearly three weeks had flown by since Bagshorne had led me to White Horse farm—and Philomela. "Philomela"—what a sweet name it was, and how well suited! Of course I loved her, and had done so, I think from the moment I had seen the tumbled glory of her hair and the laughter deep within her eyes. Ah, yes, she had wonderful eyes whose very mischief puzzled me. Often when talking with her their thick lashes would lift unexpectedly, and I would find them regarding me with a look that belied her serious mouth.

What was it about me, I wondered, that she found so inextinguishably humorous? Well, what matter? I would be going soon, and these three weeks filled in with the whisper of golden corn, the plash of brooks, and the sighing of wind in trees would remain for me a memory wherein Philomela would stand proud and tall as I had first seen her, with sunbeams in her hair. Hereupon, having finished dressing, I sighed and threw open the casement. As I leaned there, the fragrance of the morning about me, I arrived at a sudden determination. After all—I told myself—a man's personal happiness was entirely his own affair. What could my respected governor know of such things. I would act for myself, despite his confounded strong-minded-ness, and as for Miss Esther Clarges—bah!

I made my way downstairs and out into the sunshine with a new feeling of exhilaration upon me. As I turned into the paddock I was surprised to see Bagshorne sitting upon a gate. He did not notice me as I approached, and I saw for a wonder that he was without his pipe. Instead, he held his watch in his hand, from which his glance wandered to a certain wing of the house every half second or so. Also he had a hoe balanced across his knees.

"Hallo, Bagshorne!" I cried as I came up. "Thought you were in bed."

"Well, I'm not," he said shortly.

"But what on earth are you doing with that hoe?" I inquired.

Bagshorne looked uncomfortable, and made an involuntary movement to do the impossible and hide it with his coat.

"Nothing," he answered. "That is," he continued, smiling feebly, "thought I'd do a little hoeing, you know."

I grinned.

"Hang it," he exclaimed, trying to carry it off with a high hand. "I suppose there's nothing to prevent a fellow doing a bit of hoeing if he wants to?"

"Certainly not," I returned, "only I didn't know you were fond of that sort of—"

"Shut up!" he interrupted, and as he spoke a gate creaked and I saw Betty Carlyon coming toward us.

"Oh," she cried, "you are both here! Mr. Bagshorne," she continued, looking at me with eyes full of laughter, "has taken advantage of this lovely morning to get up early—he hates getting up early, you understand." Bagshorne attempted a feeble denial.

"And," she went on, "he has promised to show me how to hoe turnips."

"Really," I said, "I'd no idea hoeing was one of his accomplishments. He is, I fear, given to hiding his light under a bushel."

"I think you might profit by so excellent an example," she laughed, "and try to make yourself useful too."

"Delighted," I answered, " if I knew where—"

"In the dairy," she said, and turned away with a smiling nod.

Bagshorne's idea of carrying a hoe is quaint. It seemed to worry him. I believe he would have thrown it away had he dared. I watched until a hedge hid them from sight, and then directed my footsteps toward the dairy. Yet for some reason, as I drew nearer, I began to hesitate: A dairy, after all, is so distinctively a woman's province, so to speak. Thus, in a state of weak vacillation, I skirmished round for some time. Once I paused to listen to a distant peal of silvery laughter. I knew what that meant—Bagshorne was hoeing! I would have given a great deal to see him at that moment.

The dairy forms one of the many outbuildings, and is lighted by three windows. Working my way from one to the other, I presently came to the door and, leaning there, looked in. The sun shone strong behind me, casting my shadow along the tiled floor to where Philomela stood with her back to me busy at the churn. Thus she presently turned and saw me. Her wilful hair had come loose and hung low upon her neck, and her cheeks were flushed with her exertions.

"Oh!" she said in a tone of surprise, "you are down early."

"Yes. I wanted to—to talk to you."

Philomela shook her head.

"I'm much too busy," she answered, and stooped over a low, wide pan of milk, doing something mysterious with a long-handled arrangement I could make nothing of.

"I won't take a minute, if you'll only listen," I said persuasively.

"Well?" And all in a moment she turned and faced me, looking at me with the same puzzling half-veiled merriment in her eyes.

"Well?" she repeated.

"Oh!" I stammered, taken aback by the suddenness of it, "I—I merely wished to know if you would care—that is, if you would be good enough to—to marry me?"

Philomela turned away, and there was a pause during which I felt supremely conscious that my speech had not been as impressive as I had intended.

"I've loved you ever since I first saw you," I pursued, "and couldn't go away without telling you. Will you marry me, dear?"

"No, I won't " she answered without looking round. I had felt it was hopeless all along, but something in her manner, something in the way she said it, with her back turned to me, filled me with an uneasy surprise.

"Will you tell me why?" I asked.

"Because yours is a nature to which the idea of marriage, even in the vaguest, most abstract form is—"

"Where—where did you hear that?" I faltered.

"Wholly abhorrent," she went on, "and surely you wouldn't advise a girl to marry a man who is 'morally unfitted—'"

"Where—tell me, Philomela, where did you hear all that—foolery?"

She turned slowly without speaking and held out a letter.

"Why—this—I—I wrote this to a Miss Esther Clarges," I stammered.

"Well! I am Esther Clarges."

"You! But—Philomela! 'Philomela'!"

"'Philomela' was Harold's idea," and she turned back to the milk pans.

"I think I'd better go," I said at last.

"I told you I was very busy," she answered. So, without another word, I turned and left her and with a set purpose directed my way toward the turnip field. Presently I spied Bagshorne sitting under a hedge, alone. His pipe was in his mouth and his hoe lay neglected beside him.

"Ah!' said he as I approached, "have *you* quarreled too?"

"Look here, Bagshorne," I began, "why did you let me write that accursed letter?"

"Accursed letter?" he repeated. "You've found out then, Ah, well! Well, I advised you not to send it, you know."

"Why." I continued, "did you allow me to think that she was a middle-aged spinster without an idea above a pig? Why didn't you tell me that Esther Clarges was your cousin?"

"If you come to think of it," said he, in his idiotic way, "you never asked me. Thought I'd let you find out for yourself."

"Well," I said bitterly, "you may care to know that you've ruined my life."

Bagshorne actually chuckled. "Bad as that, is it! She refused you, I suppose?"

"Absolutely," I said, checking a fierce impulse to strike him severely with his own hoe.

"Of course—quite natural. You asked her to, you know. But," he continued, pausing to blow out a cloud of smoke, "did she say she didn't love you?"

"Why, no," I answered, staring at him with a new hope dawning.

"Then suppose you go back and ask her," he suggested.

"Bagshorne—do you really think—"

"Never mind what I think. Just take my advice for once, and go and ask her."

I went, and five minutes later was back in the dairy.

"You've not gone, then?" she said, interrogating me with a quick side glance.

"No—I want to know if you love me, Esther?"

"I don't quite see what that has to do with one who is 'morally unfitted—'"

"Tell me," I insisted, but she went on skimming without answering for quite a long while, until I took her hand in mine, skimmer and all.

"Do—you," she began hesitatingly, "love Esther so much that you would have married Philomela, in spite of—of your 'Roman parent'?"

"All the strongest-minded 'Roman fathers' in the world would not have stopped me," I answered, stooping until I could see her eyes.

"Then—" she began, and stopped.

"Well?" I asked, stooping lower, and although her lips were silent I read my answer in the sudden swift droop of her lashes.

"Do you know, Dick," she said, after a while, "we have a great deal to thank Harold for. We understand each other so much better than if—"

"Bagshorne is a good chap," I answered. "The very best of good chaps—and I'll write to that Roman governor of mine tomorrow."

His reports on the Dempsey-Carpentier championship fight in 1921 had enhanced Jeffery Farnol's reputation as a lay expert on 'The Noble Art.' He had confirmed this with his well-researched book on famous prize fights, 'Epics of 'The Fancy', which appeared in 1928, built around a series of boxing articles that had appeared a year earlier in 'The Weekly Despatch.' So this article, written for the London 'Evening Standard' of July 26, 1928, came as no surprise to his reading public.

THESE MILLION-DOLLAR FIGHTS

The Last of Them? No, Not While Boxing Stands for Big Business.

Mr Gene Tunney, the present and perhaps most original of all the heavy-weight champions of the world, is reported to have said that his match with Tom Heeney to-night will be the last of these million-dollar fights; the which dictum, I, for one, here and now humbly beg leave to doubt.

For, as it seems to me, the human animal is a creature so strangely constituted that if he be forbidden a certain thing, or charged a ridiculous and prohibitive price therefor, he will instantly put upon that same thing an extravagant value and burn with a fierce ardour for its attainment at any price and at all hazards.

Our world's champion is also reported to have said (though what a champion is and says must prove very often a great shock for that same champion to read)—our champion says then, that he is not in the boxing game because he likes it, but for the reason, and a very sufficient and sensible reason it surely is, that it has been proved a highly paying business.

And there it is!

The word "business" itself explains many things, since business is at odds with sport, is indeed its very opposite and always must be.

Thus today a world's champion is, and I suppose, through stress of circumstances must be, an extremely business-like business man, who, as a rule, to carry on his business, finds it necessary to employ a huge staff of lesser business men, agents, secretaries, log-rollers, and what not; he and they, with their eyes upon the main chance, think always in terms of money and talk lightly of money in stupendous sums.

The Syndicate.

Indeed, a world's champion is a capitalist and may earn in one year as much or more than any successful barrister or doctor can acquire in a whole lifetime of studious devotion to his profession. But then, and forsooth, a modern World's Championship Prize Fight is become a huge commercial undertaking, the exploitation of brawn and skills not by and for themselves and the glory of it, but rather by a syndicate of hard-headed business-men hot and eager for their percentages.

Hence to settle the articles of the Great Affair requires the presence of divers men of the law, etc., and the contract is drawn up with all the dignity and painful care of any other great business deal.

Veterans of the Ring Side, looking wistfully backward across the years, compare our modern pugilist, more or less ironically, with champions of the past, when boxers contended for glory as much as for money, and took a pride in their hard-smiting trade.

In those simpler, less comfortable days of our grandsires lived champions who drew no line, evaded no opponents, but welcomed all and sundry, nor bargained for a fortune before they could be induced to toss their castors into the ring.

Also, in those Spartan days, to see a fight of champions one generally had to walk very far, ride very hard, or journey by coach or crawling, crowded train, and thereafter trudge weary miles away to some sequestered greensward selected with extraordinary care in order to baffle interruption by the authorities.

Fugitive Days.

Boxing was indeed one of the fugitive sports in that unenlightened age, and therefore much cherished. It was of the sun and wind and open spaces

To-day, for those blessed with much worldly goods, to witness a championship fight is as prosaic, for the most part, in almost every way, as attending a theatre, and generally as comfortable.

Now, this being the Age of Mammon, I venture to set down this question, to wit: Were two super-champions to fight for the title and a crown of parsley, would their efforts be watched by as many wide, eager eyes as would be the struggle of two lesser men who battled for a million dollars? I wonder!

So it is that million-dollar fights are with us and, I venture to think, will remain.

For, so long as there are business men with an eye to the main chance and writers to pen the praises of these more or less famous modern gladiators, to tickle the ears of their readers with pungent criticism and anecdote concerning them, so long will million-dollar fights endure. For we mere ordinary folk, fired by these lurid reports, shall kick off our slippers, quit our cosy fire-sides, and flock in our jostling thousands to pay our humble Bradbury, and all to behold that which the great majority of us have usually not the least interest in, or of which we have not the slightest understanding.

Yet being upon the place of combat, we sit enthralled while two men (seen afar, and whom we know not at all save by reading and hearsay) pound and pommel each other.

Wondering.

Crouched thus upon an uncomfortable perch, we gaze forgetful of ourselves, of our troubles, and all save those two dominant, heroical figures in the roped arena; and setting our hearts and sympathies upon one of them, we flinch to every resounding, painful wallop, we gasp, we cheer, we groan, till finally, rejoicing in the victory or sorrowing in the defeat of our chosen man, home we go again amazed at ourselves and wondering "what it was all about".

But we have had a remarkable experience after all, since we have seen two men fight for and one man win (in an incredibly short space of time), a sum of money, nay, a very fortune, that to us mere ordinary human beings is, alas, far, far beyond our utmost dreams.

In 1933 the Great Depression was raging; like many others, Jeffery Farnol was feeling its effects. He was approached, and agreed, to write the foreword for a 100-page promotional booklet for the seaside resort of Hove, Sussex, close to his home at 'Sunnyside'. The result follows. To me, it is almost a parody of his writing style; but the Hove publicity department probably felt that they had more than got what they'd paid for. I transcribed this piece from Farnol's original manuscript, meticulously written in ink in a schoolboy's exercise book that sold for 2d. Throughout the whole, I doubt whether there were more than half a dozen author's corrections.

HOVE

WHEN Man came up from the abysmal darkness, one of his first instincts was to provide himself and progeny with a shelter from the elements; next, a defence against foes; and lastly, as his intelligence increased, with the comforts of a home. To which purpose he chose as his abiding place such sites as were best to his liking and which he deemed the most salubrious.

And Hove, Hova or Hoove (for through the dusty ages its name shows variously spelled) has been such an abiding place since those far off, misty days when Man went armed with club or flint-axe and himself bedight in skins of bear, deer, sheep and otter.

For Hove, lying between flower-sprent Down and teeming sea, was a place of health even then, its life-giving soil being watered by sweet rills and pellucid rivers, and famous, far and wide, for its magic spring. Wherefore, to Hove came barbarian Kings and great chieftains to live their wild lives in this vicinage and, eventually, to die and be buried here in the great mound or tumulus that once stood a few yards from the Church of St. John at the north of Palmeira Square; which ancient barrow being removed to make way for certain shops, yielded up divers interesting relics and among them a cup of amber wondrously fashioned, a treasure almost unique as an archaeological find and now the most valued possession of the Brighton Corporation. (But why and wherefore Brighton? says I.) Hove, to be sure, has a model of this priceless cup that was once the treasured possession of some British King or mighty chieftain, for only a person of high distinction could have owned such rarity which, having been a joy to him in life, was buried with his noble and honoured bones.

Thus, then, it is fairly evident that Hove was a place of some importance in the hazy days of those strange, warlike, mysterious folk with their druids, their mistletoe, their sacred oak-groves and sacrifices (those terrible wicker cages) that we are wont to call the Early Britons.

Then the Romans, those wise and wonderful folk, were quick to recognise the virtues of this place; so in Hove, and round about, they built them pleasant villas and a town, the memory of which is long out of mind though their sites have been determined and broken fragments of their past splendours found from time to time. For alas, after Roman law and peace had endured some while, Chaos rushed, a fierce wave of ruthless Barbarism to ravage and waste, destroying all those wonders of craftsmanship that were far beyond the understanding of poor, blind Savagery.

But then came the mighty Saxon with longsword and double-bladed war-axe to bring order anew: to plough and sow here in sea-girt Sussex, to reap and mow these lush meads and long, green slopes, and so to become a great people.

At Eastdean and Westdean, in one-time sleepy Alfriston we have found many traces of our stout Saxon fore-fathers—ones long in arm and thigh, with beads, brooches, spear-heads, swords; often he lies with his great bi-pennis war-axe beside him, guarding, as it were in death, the rich heritage his valour won for him so many years ago.

In Hove itself, not so long since, there was unearthed such a warrior with shield, spear and seax; his once-stalwart bones crumbled back to goodly dust, almost at once, but his weapons remain and are to be seen today in Hove Museum by any such as shall take the trouble.

Doubtless in the Saxon hamlet of Hove was sound of terror, groans of men, cries and wailing of fearful children and women, on that black day for Saxon England, when in this fair Sussex, and dreadfully near, King Harold's bejewelled Dragon Banner tottered and fell upon the trampled bloody mire and littered slopes above wide Pevensey Level when, as night came down, the Norman battle-cry rang, hoarse, faint yet triumphant, and the waters of Sangue-lac were red with blood indeed at last, according to the ancient prophecy of Merlin.

So, through the long years, while generations came and went, while little England grew and waxed in might and greatness, little Hove persisted through good times and bad, through report equally good and evil, now a sleepy hamlet, a flourishing fishery village,—again almost a desolation, its two aged churches fallen to ruin, its wide, lonely beaches the wild haunt of screaming seagull and silent smuggler. There are (or lately were) two sleepy old cobblestone cottages at the end of Hove Street, might, and they could, have told strange, wild tales of windy darkness and the "gen'lemen o' the night" with their strings of shaggy ponies heavy laden with keg and bale, flitting like shadows, darker than the dark, by desolate ways and lonely tracks and with never a sound save a furtive click of hoof-iron or tramp of unwary foot, stealing by, all ware and watchful, to hide those same kegs and bales in such unlikely places as graves, ancient tombs, the crypts and even pulpits of lonely churches, and, of course, in the goodly chalk. There is, or was, a chalk pit at the junction of Sackville and Old Shoreham roads where, some few years since, was discovered a series of caves, hewn by the hand of man who shall say when or to what purpose? But assuredly used by his descendants to defraud his then Majesty's Government of its somewhat too heavy imposts.

Thus rolled the years, and little Hove, of small account until in the 18th century, some bright soul rediscovered what his ancestors, Early British, Roman, Saxon and Norman, had known so very well, that this spot of earth called Hove, this poor fishing village whose men folk were busiest at night, fishing kegs and what not from their buoyed and hidden moorings,—that this poor, seemingly-insignificant place was rich in health-giving properties and possessed of a Magic Spring whose waters wrought marvellously within the human frame. So they dubbed this so ancient spring St. Ann's Well and flocked thereunto daily, on two legs, four legs and rattling wheels, to drink amain of its curative, revitalizing waters.

Not content with this, many there were (moneyed folk, of course) who built houses to be ever near these blessed waters and to breathe the sweet, life-giving air of Hove.

Thus the little, fishing, smuggling hamlet of Hove passed away; this small, neglected, down-at-heel Hove that had viewed so long with awe and wonder its modish, touch-me-not neighbour, the very dashing, politely raffish Brighthelmstone, the prosperous, consciously superior Brighton,—Hove began to stir at last, to stretch and, fully waking, found herself almost beautiful and growing ever more so. For to-day where Brighton swaggers, jovially genteel, Hove shows graciously demure, of a spacious, somewhat conscious stateliness with her noble squares and broad, sunny avenues trending from busy thoroughfare and goodly shops to the open sea. A truly domestic place is Hove, where the weary paterfamilias home returning from busy London street and office, breathes deep of a sweet and vital air and, scarce knowing why, is glad.

Also in Hove, with the sole exception of the Race Course, you shall find every other sport. Would you behold famous wielders of the willow, here is the County Cricket Ground; or watch lithe athletes chase the leathern sphere,—in Hove is the best football arena in the County. Would you in one sense go to the dogs, they too are here to your joyous profit or loss.

Would you bathe? Then choose but your time and any of her many beaches and you have the safest water anywhere to be found in this round earth; and, your bathing done, what joy inexpressible to lie outstretched upon a sun-kissed pebble ridge and feel a gentle though vital warmth steal through and through your grateful body, inducing such voluptuous well-being as shall make you joy to be blessed with life.

Are you of reverent, enquiring mind? Would you glimpse and see perhaps age-old wonders, the dim footsteps of your long-forgotten ancestry?

Then, 0 Brother, come you to Hove. And now, together, afoot or awheel, let us away East, West, or North, where these marvels lie for us, waiting to be found and, as I fancy, eager to be looked at by such as are of reverent mind and are blessed with mental sight, those wonderful Eyes of the Mind that may envision so much.

See now, Brother, Northward before us sweep the Downs, range on range of tender beauty, far as sight may reach,—the vivid green of sun-kissed summits, the sombre shades of grassy ravine and bush-grown declivity, fading afar to lavender, purple and blue until these pale to the vague distances.

And, moreover, in these immemorial Downs doth lie much of this small, mighty island's inspiring history; upon and about these silent, grassy slopes, long-forgotten peoples lived and loved, fought, died and lie buried in the white chalk, their winding-sheet this virgin, velvet sward, thick-sown with dancing scabious and a myriad other tinier flowerets.

See yonder! Lift up your eyes where the grassy ridge shows so purely plain against the blue. "A turfy mound?" says you. Yea, brother, the last bed of some long-forgotten King or mighty man, become now goodly dust and integral part of this England he loved, and for which he lived, so many weary years ago. Yes, there he lies on couch uplift towards heaven yet within sight of the English sea,—what bed for an Englishman! May he sleep well whosoever he was.

Tumuli, Brother? They are all about you, with Ancient British fortified villages and Roman Camps and townships,—squares, circles and ellipses, no more than turfy mounds to-day, I grant you, but open your Mind's Eyes and vision them as they were,—vallum and fosse, tower and wall and gate, all glad and noisy with life or grimly silent and sternly a-glitter for defensive battle. Battle? Sir, I tell you there is no single foot of all these gentle slopes but has been fought over time and again, has known the victor's fierce joy with the bitter agony of death and vanquishment.

Yes, they are all about you, waiting to greet you perhaps as a descendant of themselves, these strange, wild folks so very dead and forgotten yet once so very much alive, who lived and died upon these sunny highlands all around us. Hearken now to the names of them: Thunder-barrow Hill. The Devil's Dyke. Edburton Camp. Buckland Bank. Hollingbury Ring. Wolstonbury Circle. Ditchling Beacon. Sompting. Whitehawk Camp. Thus for the Highlands,—these senior embattled villages and townships the youngest of which numbers more than a thousand years. Now for the juniors, the Lowland villages and hamlets: Beeding, Bramber, Fulking, Poynings,—Brother, do you hear them? Don't they come to you like the ring of clarions and trumpets out of the long ago, touching some till-now forgotten chord within your being that makes you know beyond all doubt that, like the mighty dust within these ancient barrows, the living turf that springs beneath your unwearied tread, that you are one with it all, a present, living part of this hoary, old England with a stake in her and all her noble traditions?

What's over there? Golf, old fellow, yea, and all you will. For almost in sight from this lofty eminence are nine clubs devoted to the Royal and ancient game—nine, Brother, no less! Off yonder across from old Hollingbury is to be had another Royal pastime, for there is the Brighton Race Track for this sport of Kings, whereby so many that are nowise kingly wax prosperous and plethoric....Far better go a-fishing, at least, so think I. Yes, indeed, for with a book of "marks," a boat and company of one who knows the water hereabouts, you shall not cast line or twiddle rod in vain. An outfit? Most certainly, Hove shall supply your every need from lugworm to motor-boat. Eh, you'd prefer a gallop on the Downs? A horse? Brother, for reasonable fee you shall be mounted like a paladin and ride with a fragrant wind, twixt Downland and the sea, upon those lost roads and dim seen tracks where your ages-forgotten kinsfolk galloped their shaggy steeds.

Are you a father and dutifully conscious of your responsibilities? Here for your children be pleasant lagoons of sufficient though quite undrownable depths whereon small boats ply for small hire, dainty craft self-propelling, screw and paddle, wherein happy youngsters may be their own engines, and eke navigators, until they weary themselves comfortably to the accompaniment of martial music discoursed, near and far, by the bands of divers celebrated regiments.

Or again; would you ply the nimble racquet? Lo! you, here are courts a-many, grass and hard, whereon you may bound and leap, drive, volley and smash, your heated brow fanned meantime by gentle zephyrs from the sea that ebbs and flows within a scant few yards; and hereafter, being dowered of a noble thirst you may assuage it promptly in adjacent café or, seeking more Easterly, quaff a foaming flagon in a cool, shady interior worthy the drinking of goodly ale, looking forth upon that part of the sea front where his late Majesty King Edward VII was wont to stride to and fro, morning and evening, because the air he breathed and the earth he trod was Hove.

Are you a dressy man with handsome wife or beautiful daughter? Tread you then the carefully-tended, velvet sward of the Brunswick Lawns and there display your splendours, for there indeed Fashion and Beauty are wont to parade, more especially of a Sunday.

Thus Hove, growing ever more alluring, in dignified stately fashion, is certainly a place where Mr. Everyman and his lady may tarry awhile to the betterment of their physical welfare, nor weary while this betterment is a-doing. Hove indeed, like the lady (and woman of the world) she has become, is ready to welcome all and sundry and to do her best for them and with them, that she may.

And what of myself, says you?

Well, Brother, seeing I live hereabouts and love this beautiful, gentle Sussex, its quaint folk, its honoured traditions and countless age-old associations—should the weather be rough, there is for me a peaceful room, a deep arm-chair, a seasoned briar and an unfinished book. But, if Old Sol smile, I know a grassy nook, just this side of the Devil's Dyke, whence the happy eye may behold a wide stretch of Downland, hill and dale, flash of limpid stream and shadow of darkling wood with here and there a bowery village a-peep mid the green of aged trees: Here throned, I shall smoke and look and dream of the long vanished folk who lived hereabout in other days when England was rising upon the world and waxing ever mightier; when this world itself was simpler and living a more thoughtful, leisured business, with no roaring rush of speeding aeroplane or scurry and racket of hooting motors; and perhaps in the many unseen presences that surely haunt these solitudes, more especially in the hush of evening and the awesome approach of night, I shall feel again, as I so often do, the old, great quietude, the deep, solemn, slow-moving soul of Old England that, of its simple, homely faith and commonsense wisdom (which is perhaps the highest of all wisdom) has in the past taught the world so very much. From the dark merciless age, whose cruelty inspired Magna Carta and Habeas Corpus to the now so mocked and contemned era of Victoria when Britain's prestige stood so superlatively high, Old England has led through the tears and blood of her own suffering onward and upward as so, pray God, I dare to dream, she may do yet.

And when my pipe is out and my dreaming done, I shall turn my face to the sea that was Old England's power, and going homeward, shall thank God for this wide Downland country and the sweet and gentle peace of it in this rushing, sorely troubled world; and looking from these green highlands down on Hove, shall be thankful for it, as I ever am, and for the vital air I breathe.

Jeffery Farnol (compiled and edited by Pat Bryan) • 85

So, Brothers all, would ye find a part of England, old and new, that shall fit your every mood and need,—come ye to Hove.

Jeffery Farnol wrote easily and swiftly, although he was always a consummate craftsman, and would revise extensively if he was dissatisfied with what he had written the night before. This short verse was a petit jeu d'esprit *written to amuse his wife Phyllis, affectionately know as 'Pilk'. She obviously enjoyed it enough to keep it; and for all that it was dashed off in the wee small hours, its rhyming and scansion are impeccable, and the language is pure Farnol.*

TO MY SPOUSE—OUR PILK

My Dearest, Knowing that I oughter
Check that distressing flow of water
I fared me forth into the night
And by a taper's twinkling light
Beyond the garage gates; I found
'Neath iron lid, deep in the ground
I say, beneath this iron trap
By taper's light, I saw—a tap.
This tap, while fitful taper burned
This tap in trap, deftly I turned
This tap, by taper's flickering light
I turned and turned, from left to right;
Turned, my dear, to such effect
That I the spouting torrent checked.
Thus when you for the plumber send
To mend whatever is to mend
Inform him how your spouse last night
With merest taper's dismal light
Like hero in lone midnight, sought
And with that tap, so ably wrought.

Which tap turned off, turned on must be
Till water spout again that he
May find thus what he has to do.
And so Sweet Spouse, Goodnight to you
For now, my PILK with silent tread
I'll crawl and creep me up to bed
Stealthy crawl and silent creep
Lest trouble I thy balmy sleep
So snore, spouse, snore and slumbrous lie
Snore thy best and so will I.

Note on awakening!
Left by Jack Jeffery Farnol.
(Phyllis's notation)

On Christmas Eve, 1944, the 'Sunday Empire News', a jingoistic Conservative English newspaper, featured on its editorial page a series of hopeful articles anticipating the end of the war in Europe, which would happen less than six months later. There were letters from the publishers of major newspapers in Canada, Australia, New Zealand, South Africa and other parts of the British Empire. There was an article about the true meaning of Christmas by the Rev. Dr. W.E.Sangster, a prominent non-conformist cleric. There were cautionary articles about the need to work for a lasting peace, and the likelihood of post-war turmoil throughout Europe. And the lead article was written by Jeffery Farnol, and titled 'Merry England in Brave New Days.' It took up two columns of the entire seven-column page, and featured an informal photograph of Jeffery, his wife Phyllis, and a twelve-year old Jane with her father's arm around her shoulders.

MERRY ENGLAND IN BRAVE NEW DAYS

This being an age when the old, simple beliefs of our ancestors are frowned upon or condemned by partially-educated Commonsense, and ourselves dazzled by scientific marvels, is also the age of bombs and doodle-bugs with other Teutonic deviltries of an obscene brutality and blindly-wanton destruction unparalleled in all the long dark history of Man's slow ascent from the primordial Beast.

And so, as yet another Christmas draws near, we, the war-worn, are sad of heart and woefully bewildered of mind by this senseless waste and indescribable suffering wrought by a Science wielded by and prostituted to such atrocious Evil.

Troubled thus for our long-vaunted civilisation and sickened by the depths to which intellect and a misused science have plunged us, what wonder if we sigh for a simpler world and turn from the ghastly present to peer back wistfully through the dust of hurrying centuries to that fabled Golden Age called "The Good Old Days"?

So now, while earth and sky and sea are filled with the hellish roar of merciless conflict and death's grim angel hovers so near us all, glance we back to a far saner though perhaps less heroic Christmas when peace blessed this now troubled earth and men (for a brief while at least) were joined in a great Brotherhood of Goodwill.

"Ye Good Olde Days"

At Christmastide in the Good Old Days, this "Merrie England" of ours grew so very much the merrier and more jovial, greeting this glad festival of the Nativity with such joy of singing and rapturous clamour of bells, such dancing and feasting that perhaps because of this cheery freedom and hearty good fellowship, these times became known as "The Good Olde Days".

And such truly they must have been (for the happy few) when in noble hall, stately bower and cosy homestead the Yule log blazed upon wide and open hearths; when, mellowed by this ruddy fire-glow, torch, cresset, candle or lamp, beamed upon happy faces thronged above hospitable board or well-laden table brave with right lusty fare. Ho, for the smoking barons of juicy beef! For huge hams pinkly succulent! For mighty neat's tongues richly spiced! For vasty boar's heads fiercely tusked yet luscious and savoury to both eye and nose.

Verily these were the good old days, my masters, when flagons, beakers and blackjacks, cups or glasses brimmed with foaming ale, mead, cider, perry or rich wines from beyond seas. Yea faith, right merry days, for the chosen, happy few! But how of the woeful many?

Yonder in walled city and fortified township, amid the maze of crooked, sunless streets and narrow alleys, in foul dens, noisome cellars and crowded rookeries, Misery and Famine crouch side by side with Disease and slow-creeping Death. Upon desolate high road and shadowy bye lane, murder leaps to smite and rob; men kill that they may live, the hungry steal that they may eat, yet soon or late are hunted to gallows and gibbet, be their sinning great or small. Thus in the old criminal records we may read of a young mother hanged for theft of a sixpenny handkerchief.

For alas! In those Good Old Days that are now, thank God, so far behind us, starvation was accounted a necessary evil, a mysterious dispensation of Providence and duly accepted as such, since, according to Holy Writ: "The poor ye have always with you".

Thus so late as the Year of Grace, 1857, in a certain great London journal still extant, we may read with terrible frequency and set down with a more terrible indifference, brief accounts of poor, solitary creatures found dead for mere lack of a crust, while the great city's many church bells pealed glad welcome to the advent of another Happy Christmas.

Yet our Old England marched on, merry of heart, on and up through painful years, thriving despite iniquitous laws, pestilence, internal strife and plague of war, growing ever mightier because the struggling soul of her was clean and by instinct she loved the good, great things—justice and liberty—with an invincible devotion that, mighty in endurance, defied prison, torture, the headsman's axe, and won to freedom in and through the fires of Smithfield.

Thus grew our Merry England, making a joke of hardship and peril, smiling cheerily in the grim face of disaster, saving a great army and thereafter the world itself when there was no hope or help but God alone; doing the impossible as a matter of course and with no braggadocio flourish of trumpet or beat of drum; daring all despite all, Old England has endured, though often her merriment has been somewhat grim.

Never So Glorious…

Through the mud and blood of stricken France, through bullet-swamps and jungles of Burma her sons have fought and joked their resistless way, victors certain of final conquest because of themselves so very sure. Truly a breed the like of which can be found only in this small, sea-lashed isle.

To all of us, here in war-torn England, this must needs be a lean Christmas, for many of us a season of grievous sorrow, for none of us a truly glad festival. But surely never since the first Christmas dawned has there been one so glorious as in this Year of God, 1944.

And this because through the thinning reek of this foul war, across the cruel waste of shattered homes and scarred earth, eyes though misted with tears may yet glimpse a fitful beam, a growing light that is the now certain dawn of victory, the very Peace of God and therewith, I pray, a happier, nobler world.

In the Good Old Days our forefathers were wont to sing at Christmas: *"God rest ye, merry gentlemen, May nothing you dismay"*

But I dare to think that in ages to come our descendants, looking back at this woeful year from a far better world, may describe and hail these our years of tribulation as:

"The Brave Old Days—when Britain alone, deserted, hard beset and sore wounded, fronted all the pitiless might of the unconquered Beast and saved the world—alone, yet high of heart, steadfast and undismayed because—alone with God."

"Whom Nothing Could Dismay"

And now, as this most glorious Christmas draws near, I like to believe how at such seasons hereafter these happier generations yet to be, for whose sake we of to-day suffer and endure, may amend the old song, perhaps something like this: *"God saved those merry Gentlemen, Whom nothing could dismay"*

Thus I who pen these lines, loving our Merry England and proud to be of her so faithful, much-enduring folk, can think of no better Christmas greeting than that:

God may still bless our England
And her children every one;
That she for right may fearless stand
So long as time shall run.

This essay, a mere 270 words long, is undated, although it most likely is from the period just after the end of the Second World War. Some of its phrases seem almost Chestertonian in their paradoxity. I don't recognise it as being from one of Farnol's books, and the fact that it had been typed with its own title suggests that it is a stand-alone piece.

FEAR

Fear, that shapeless monster rising out of the dark realms of an undisciplined imagination, hurling Reason from her throne and flooding the senses in a rampant riot of pervading mastery. A creeping, insinuating presence, that, out of nothingness creates giant phantoms, and peoples the darkness with looming, sinister horrors, turns the very silence into a menacing expectation wherein the creak of a board is more potent than a clap of thunder and tears the wrought nerves with a relentless cruelty.

Fear, crouched in the blackest corner will change the innocent nook into a very crater of hell wherein lurk the watchful, mal-formed sons of darkness, waiting their chance to creep forth unseen, and, in their awful grasp, drag us with them forever down into the devastating regions of eternal terror. Or, creeping into the innocent folds of a suspended gown, will invest the gentle lines with an eerie power and hateful suggestiveness of a hidden, evil personality dominating the lifeless thing, changing its shape with a stealthy bulge here, a ghastly indentation there, until we close our eyes and wait helplessly to be enfolded in the clammy inertia of those lank and strangely contorted sleeves.

Fear, like genius, stultifies the other senses; it is an excess of imagination and feeds thereon. If encouraged it will grow to a veritable monster, destroying sanity and reign supreme, conjuring forth from shapeless nothings, dark horrors that fill the brain and elude the eye, carrying the mind into a land of shadowed evils where the comfort of Reason is not known.

I can find no record of this poem ever having been published. It was among a number of papers sent to me by noted Farnol fan Robert Ellenwood; he had probably obtained the original from Phyllis Farnol, Jeffery's second wife, when he visited her in Eastbourne in 1980. As mentioned at the end of the poem, it was written in Cornwall, at 'The Anchorage', Portscatho, to where the Farnols had evacuated to escape the worst of the bombing of England's South coast. The poem obviously salutes the sufferings of London during the Blitz.

OLD LONDON TOWN

Ho, London, loved and famous London Town:
Augusta, with thy bruised and battered crown.
Old London, with thy scars upon thy brow,
Crowned with new glory everlasting;—thou
May'st look back through a thousand crowded years
Of good and evil, grief, and joy and tears.
Briton and Roman, Saxon, Norman, Dane;
Battle and plague, deep loss and mighty gain.
Thou hast known blackest shame and brightest glory,
But never such in all thy wondrous story
As when all hell its fury on thee hurled,
And made of thee a flame to light the world.
A flame, a fire, that purged away thy dross,
And showed a figure nailed upon a cross.
Oh, London, shrine thou of our mighty dead
Thrice hallowed now by blood so lately shed;
By this, great city of our love and pride,
To England's Sons thou art now sanctified.
Thy poorest, meanest streets are hallowed all;

Thy very name, like ringing bugle call,
Cries "Hope," and doth Hope's rousing message bear
To nations thralled, and lost in black despair.
Rouse ye! Wake ye, and new courage take;
The dawn of freedom soon shall on thee break.
God is not mocked; Christ suffered not in vain;
Redemption cometh; ye shall live again.

Today, Old London, nobler is thy fame,
For blessed hope sings in thy spoken name.
Today the wounds are now for us to see,
But for the generations yet to be
When Life's great wheel hath turned folk then shall say:
"Oh, to have lived in London in that day
When she, death's anguished path for freedom trod,
Alone in all the world:—alone with God,
When London's children, fronting shock and flame
In London died, to win the world from shame.
Thus London, with thy scarred and battered brow,
Greater, nobler, holier yet art thou.
Thy name henceforth shall inspiration be,
To reach from pole to pole and sea to sea:"

JEFFERY FARNOL In Cornwall, 1943.

In 1944, the Features Editor of the 'Daily Mail' wrote directly to Jeffery Farnol, to tell him of their plans to feature a story by a leading writer, every Saturday on the leader page. The letter continued: 'We want these stories to be the best of their kind anywhere in the world. For that reason we are writing to ask if you will contribute.' Naturally, Farnol agreed, and this story is his contribution. It appeared in the 'Mail' on Saturday, October 7, 1944. A box on the same page lists the best-sellers of the week; these include 'A King of Prussia' by Rafael Sabatini, and 'The Women's Land Army' by Vita Sackville-West.

JEFFERY FARNOL *writes this week's* **SATURDAY SHORT STORY**
This week a new story by one of the best-known exponents of the storytelling art, Jeffery Farnol. From time to time we shall return to this series started a fortnight ago and shall reprint further notable examples of the work of the world's greatest authors.

THE ROLLER

Mr Gay, big, slow-moving, and placid, was seated, pipe in mouth, on a rustic seat of his own construction, surveying in turn a large iron cylinder, a crowbar, two sacks of cement, and several lengths of flat iron, when he was roused by the sharp voice of his neighbour, Mr Fern, calling across the party wall that separated their two gardens.

"Hallo! Will—hallo! What are you up to this time?"

With his mild, blue gaze still upon the cylinder, Mr Gay replied between slow, thoughtful puffs at his well-seasoned briar: "Well, George...I'm scheming how...to make me...a lawn-roller."

"Eh—lawn-roller? But what for, seeing you've no lawn to roll? Nothing in that plot o' yours except vegetables; nary a blade of grass and not a single flower!"

"Because, George I'm…going to…lay one."

'Eh, a lawn? Why?"

"To please…my wife, George."

"But you haven't got a wife."

"No, not yet, but…she's coming."

"What—what?," snapped Mr Fern in gasping astonishment. "A wife? Marriage? No, not you—never you, Will, no, not!"

"I am committing," quoth Mr Gay ponderously, "the act of wedlock, George, nine weeks…and four days hence." Mr Fern's goggling eyes rolled in their sockets.

"Will, I would never ha' believed it of you! I'm astounded! Ah, well, one man's meat is another man's poison. Do I know the lady?"

"No you don't, George."

"And on her account you'll sacrifice your potato patch for a lawn, and make a roller out of all these oddments?"

"Ah, for her sake, George."

"It don't look possible," said Mr Fern, leaning further across the wall to survey the oddments in question. "How'll you do it, Will?"

"Well," Mr Gay explained, using pipe-stem as pointer, "I fill this iron drum with cement, ram this crowbar through it dead centre—for axle, bend these irons round each hub, bolt them together, fix a cross-bar, and the job's done."

"It'll be a pretty big roller, heavy and cumbersome, eh, Will?"

"Ar!" nodded Mr Gay, taking off his coat. "But then—so am I."

"Con-found it!" exclaimed Mr Fern pettishly, scowling heaven-wards, "it looks like rain."

"Ar!" repeated his neighbour, rolling shirt-sleeves above mighty forearms, "and wind, George."

"Oh, blast!" snarled Mr Fern. "My poor roses'll be ruined."

"But then, George, 'twill do my vegetables a power o' good."

Night brought the expected rain with a blusterous wind; but Mr Gay, oblivious to both, was busied writing, until his laborious pen was interrupted by a sudden knocking on the outer door. Slowly he lifted his great head, yet sat a while utterly motionless, gazing down wistfully at his unfinished letter; but the summons becoming louder, he rose with his usual leisured manner and, turning up the gas in the little hall, opened the door.

"Ahem! Mr Gay, I presume!" chirruped a high-pitched voice, and into the light tripped a small, shabby man who smiled and nodded, speaking in soft, cultured accents: "Hal-lo, Will! Willy boy, how de do?"

Mr Gay was dumb and seemed to become older as he stood, for his big shoulders sagged, his comely face showed suddenly lined and haggard, perceiving which his visitor tittered:

"Aha! Why so tongue-tied, Willy? Art thou speechless with pure joy at the sight of me? To be sure times are changed. You've become Mis-ter Gay, it seems. But what's in a name? You, Will, by any other name, will be as generous to your old friend Nicholas Carson for old time's sake—and your own, eh Will? So begin by inviting poor Nick in out of the rain."

"Step in," said Mr Gay obediently.

"Oho—very snug!" chirruped his visitor, glancing round the cosy sitting-room and sinking luxuriously into the deepest armchair. "You keep yourself extremely well, dear boy—I feel perfectly at home already. Do I see whisky yonder? By Ceres, I do!"

"Help yourself," said Mr Gay.

"No, ah no, Willy! If I partake, which I shall, of course, it will be far more enjoyable to be ministered unto by your good, kind self."

Dumbly obedient, Mr Gay crossed to the sideboard while his visitor, espying the unfinished letter, drew it near, scanned it, nodded, and read aloud: "'Dearest Lucy, To know you will be my wife so soon is so wonderful I can hardly believe such happiness...' And very nice too, Willy!" he tittered. "Sweet for you, and makes things easier for me."

"How so, Carson?"

"Obviously, old boy! For instance, what would your 'dearest Lucy' say if she knew her spouse-to-be was Number 402, and escaped convict—murderer?"

"Not murderer, Carson."

"Will, old man, the night you broke prison Warder Marsh was killed."

"Not by me, as well you know, Carson."

"Ay, so I do, Will, but—the police don't, the Law doesn't, and Justice is damnably blind! But the police never forget. What about that whisky, dear boy? Oh, here we are! Three fingers, Will, and just a dash of soda—thankee! As I was saying, the police never forget...a word to the nearest bobby, and—where would you be...and 'your dearest Lucy'...how then, old fellow?"

"Ruin, Carson."

"Pre-cisely!" nodded his visitor, sipping his beverage with evident enjoyment. "Thus you see how essential I am to your continued welfare. I represent freedom for you, Willy, joy and happiness for her, a glad future for Mr and Mrs Gay, all this for—a small consideration."

"Of course," nodded Mr Gay. "Blackmail."

"Oh fie, Willy! A business deal, certain regular payments for value received—"

"How much, Carson?"

"Sit down, Will, take a drink and let's discuss it like the old lags and fellow gaolbirds we are. Come and sit down!"

Slowly Mr Gay obeyed and leaning back in cushioned chair, surveyed his blackmailer with his leisured, musing gaze—the small, mean face, furtive-eyed and cruel of mouth, the puny form...Carson, keenly aware of this deliberate scrutiny, sipped, nodded, and tapping the breast of his shabby coat, murmured with his tittering laugh:

"A gun, old boy! So don't try any strong-arm nonsense! A revolver, Willy!"

"Yes," sighed Mr Gay. "I guessed it was a gun. Well…what's your price?"

I offer you two alternatives, old man; either you take me to your hearth and home as paid companion, let's say at three quid per week, all found, or board me out for six."

Mr Gay having pondered this a while, shook his head slowly, sadly, and sighed:

"Six pounds a week would beggar me."

"Well, better that, Will, than prison certainly and the rope probably for you, old man, and a broken heart for your 'dearest Lucy', poor soul! So think it over while I try another spot of your excellent whisky. Ay, and you too—fill and drink with your old gaol-chum Nick—come!"

Instead Mr Gay reached his pipe and began filling it, gazing pensively on his visitor the while, saying as he did so:

"You're not…a big man, Carson."

"True, Willy. I haven't your ponderous bulk, but I'm extremely spry and…armed remember. Ah—what are you staring at?"

"Well, Carson, I'm thinking you'd fold up small…very small."

"What the devil d'you mean?" he demanded. And, placid as ever, Mr Gay answered gently:

"I mean if you were dead."

For a breathless moment Carson starred into the good-tempered, imperturbable face opposite, then reached for his hidden weapon, but in that moment Mr Gay's big fist smote hard and true…his powerful hands became dreadfully busy.

Ensued a brief time of relentless effort, of ghastly, futile struggling—then, clutching fingers relaxed, something slithered to the floor, and lay hideously asprawl; no sound now to break the stillness save the beat of the rain upon the window, the mumble of wind in the chimney, and deep, unhurried breathing of the man who sat gazing down at his handiwork.

Gradually the rain ceased, the wind died away, but still Mr Gay sat motionless, pipe in mouth, staring down into the small, evil, direly contorted face that glared up at him with wide-starting, sightless eyes. Nor did Mr Gay rouse from his meditation until the clock struck midnight; then he sighed deeply, shook his great head distressfully and said mournfully:

"Well, Carson, you asked for it!"

"Will," said Mr Fern, leaning over the party wall in a bright, sunny morning, "that new roller o' yours is the confoundingest, loudest, squealing-and-groaningest roller that ever rolled!"

"George," answered Mr Gay, pausing in his labour to mop perspiring brow, "d'you think so?"

"I know so! Will, she's a moaning Maudie, she complains, she moans, she wails like a soul in torment! Why on earth don't you do something to stop and soothe her?"

"A soul," repeated Mr Gay, pondering the phrase, "a soul...in torment, George?"

"Yes, she's the dismalest, dolefulest roller that ever was—"

"Right you are, George—though I shouldn't call this roller a—she."

"Well, why don't you grease the thing?"

"George, I've greased it, I've oiled it, I've blackleaded it with hand unsparing, but without the least effect! Time alone can soothe and silence...a soul...in torment...I hope!"

"However," said Mr Fern, "you've laid those turves very well: it promises to be a nice lawn, Will. Your wife should be pleased when she sees it in a fortnight's time, eh, neighbour?"

"A fortnight...yes, George...I hope she will."

But in fact she never did, for a week later Mr Fern was surprised by the following letter:

Dear neighbour George,

My wife and I have decided to travel. The house and furniture are sold. To you I herewith give all my garden tools, roller included, of course, to keep you in mind of
Your friend Will.
P.S—I think the roller may act quieter for you.

Now, oddly enough, this proved to be the case, for from the hour it became Mr Fern's property the roller ceased its dismal plaints, except for an occasional groan in wet weather, and, despite its size and weight, ran so smoothly that its new owner used it frequently upon his own trim lawn, and almost as often thought upon its creator who had moved so unexpectedly and vanished without trace or sign.

Mr Fern's beautiful garden ended in a somewhat precipitous slope bounded by a stout wall, which steep Mr Fern always took care never to let his ponderous roller approach.

Not so his brawny young nephew Tom, who, upon a certain afternoon, having rolled the lawn, began rolling the neat gravel walks with youthful and joyous abandon until, coming too near the down-bending slope, the roller suddenly took charge, broke Tom's desperate hold, bounded free, and hurtled, clattering downhill.

Mr Fern, busied in distant corner, heard a terrific crash and started in alarm, heard a shout that rose to a thin scream, and, running thither, beheld nephew Tom, wide of eye and mouth agape, who pointed with wavering finger towards all that remained of the roller.

Approaching the wreckage Mr Fern checked suddenly, then shrank back appalled beyond speech—faint and sick with nauseating horror, for there amid battered and twisted iron, uprearing from shattered concrete, shaming the sunlight and fouling the very air, was something black and shrivelled and noisome, something crowned with shag of matted hair— something that had once been the small, mean head and evil face of Nicholas Carson.

Jane Farnol Curtis comments as follows: "Daddy wrote this to me in boarding school—he had been writing (books) in the kitchen by the warm stove I expect—he sometimes did—the shortages of war. He used to draw lots of little pictures sometimes through his rather rare letters." *I have taken the liberty of breaking up the poem into verses, for easier reading. The letter is dated October 23, 1944.*

A LETTER TO JANE

Dear Jane, although it's past midnight
This letter to you I must write
Because you are my darling child
And I'm your father, meek and mild.
Also because I now intend
This sketch of your BROWN dog to send
I sketched her for you, dear my daughter
Just after in my bed I'd caught her
Then she in her own bed did leap
And made pretence to be asleep
Which surely proves, as you'll agree
How very, very sly is she.

So here's the drawing, done I guess
In about 6 minutes, more or less
I had to draw so fast because
What with her head, her tail & paws
This dog of yours, Jane, never will
Keep her brown, wriggling body still.

Jeffery Farnol (compiled and edited by Pat Bryan) • 105

And now enough of her I've said
I'll of your mother tell instead.

She's very well, I'm glad to say
And growing rounder every day
Yes, every day a little plumper
Also she's knitting you a jumper
She cooks, crochets & drives the car
Sometimes near & sometimes far
She often sits and talks of YOU
She's always thinking of you too,
When up to bed she goes. I guess
She prays to God her Jane to bless
To make her brave & good that she
May each day try to better be—
Good child, sweet girl & woman who
Will make her mother happy too
And that's enough, my dear, of you.

So now, Jane, I will write of ME
And I'm as sleepy as can be
Therefore I think it will be better
If here I stop this rhyming letter
And, with my love, a 'Good Night' say
Hoping you'll do the best you may
To read all that I've written here
I've tried to write them plain, my dear
So now Good Night, upstairs I'll creep
And try to snooze & get some sleep—
Good night my dear, & once again
I pray God bless you dearest Jane.

Write you next time
To me—in rhyme.
It can't be worse
Than Father's verse
So see if you
Can make rhymes too
You will? Right ho—
To bed I'll go.

I don't know where this poem was published, although it is most likely from a local Sussex publication, and I apologize to them for my omission. The Sussex Giant or Long Man, is a presumably prehistoric figure cut into the chalk of the South Downs near Windover. Jeffery Farnol was extremely fond of the view overlooking the Giant, and his ashes were scattered there, and a bench erected in his memory in this, his favourite spot.

OUR GIANT

There stands a shape of rugged might
Hewn in the chalk, a wondrous sight,
Just where Windover's grassy height
Looks sideways to the sea.

There you shall see this Giant stand
A spear grasped in each mighty hand,
As if to guard this pleasant land
Of Sussex, by the sea.

Ages of hail and wind and rain
Have lashed and battered him in vain,
For still he stands there, bold and plain
To guard our English land.

All things have changed, as all things will,
Yet 'gainst Windover's grassy hill
Our brave, old Giant, grimly still,
Seems on his ward to stand.

But who he is, or how, or why?
Alas! None living can reply,
So many ages have sped by
Since here his makers trod.

Perhaps in days long past and dim,
After some battle fierce and grim,
The hands of warriors fashioned him
In honour of their god.

Another thought and better far,
Is: Stead of spears, like God of war,
It is the gates he holds ajar
Of immortality.

However, on this grassy steep,
Cut in the chalk so white and deep
He stands, his watchful guard to keep
O'er Sussex, by the sea.

This story, which was originally titled "A Woman's Privilege", was probably written either just before or just after Farnol arrived in New York in 1902. The manuscript, which is typed, has two return addresses on it—the first at his in-laws' home in Englewood, New Jersey, the other at 204 West 81st Street, New York City. In it, we see his penchant for using classical names for his heroines—Justinia, Philomela, Cleone, Anthea, Anticlea, Herminia and so on. The story is very lightweight, of the type that Jeffery Farnol probably found it easy to sell to the many popular magazines that were so prevalent at the time, and vastly different from his first major novel 'The Broad Highway'.

THE PRIVILEGE OF THE SEX

Justinia was angry—I could see that plainly enough.

"So you will please understand," said she over her shoulder, "the matter is settled once and for all."

I coughed. "But you may change your mind," I began.

"Never," she said firmly.

"But my dear girl," I ventured, with an attempt at the old easy assurance, "it is a woman's privilege to change her mind, and you, being a woman, you know—"

"Impossible!," she broke in, and with a little stamp of her foot this time, "my mind is firmly made up."

I shifted my position on the gate so that I could see her face.

"I have known you for six years now Justinia, and I assure you they have not been thrown away." She swept me a mocking curtsey.

"I mean," I continued loftily, "that in the time I have come to know you as no one else possibly could."

Justinia murmured something about being 'awfully clever' but I continued undisturbed: "With this knowledge to guide me I have never once pestered you with any penny-novelette business."

"In other words," I added seeing her look of surprise, "wishy-washy, sickly sentimentality, merely contenting myself with asking you to marry me."

Justinia turned away with a sudden angry gesture.

"True," I continued, seeing the movement, "I did once kiss you, but who could blame me?," and I glanced down at the straight, supple figure, and the proud face framed in sunny hair. "In fact, Justinia, I don't mind confessing the temptation is awful—now, for instance."

"If you will have the goodness to get down off that gate, I will continue my walk," she said, not deigning to notice my remark. I looked down into the lovely flushed face, and swung my legs defiantly.

"With pleasure," I answered; "but first, am I to understand that the old relations, such as they were, are to be dropped?"

"Entirely. For the future we shall ignore each other," she said stiffly.

"When do we begin?" I enquired.

"Now—at once—from this moment!"

"Then I think the best thing I can do is go abroad." She seemed to think it rather a brilliant idea. I got down off the gate, and slowly unfastened it.

"India's rather a good place for snakes and things," I remarked, as it swung open. She passed through, and stopped.

"Good-bye," she said, and held out her hand.

"Are you quite sure—" I began.

"Quite!" she answered decisively. So I sat and dangled my legs, chawing my pipe viciously, as I watched her disappear.

* * * * * * * * * * *

After mature consideration I came to the conclusion that nothing was to be gained by going abroad. Two things were mainly responsible for this decision. Firstly, India seems such a confounded distance away when one looks at it in cold blood, and secondly, as I sat in the library that evening with a map of the world before me searching for a likely spot where I might leave my bones to bleach, 'far from the madding crowd', I received a letter from Randal, asking me to his place for the shooting.

Now seeing Hunston Grange is somewhere in the wilds of Somerset and that Randal's 'shoots' were not to be 'sneezed at', I decided that India might wait a while, and accepted with a light heart. As the train steamed into Hunston station a week later, I saw Randal flourishing his whip to me from his high dog-cart.

"Come on old fellow," he yelled, "never mind your traps, leave 'em to Martin."

"Right," I exclaimed, and a few minutes later we were bowling along behind the greys, laughing and chatting like the old friends we were. A drive of a couple of miles brought us in view of The Grange, a fine old Tudor house, standing half a mile back from the road, behind an avenue of magnificent trees.

"Oh, by the way, Dick, " said Randal, linking his arm in mine as he piloted me to my room, "got a surprise for you, don't you know, wife's idea—er—knew you were rather—smitten in a certain quarter, don't you know, so we invited my cousin Justinia, wife's idea," he continued, triumphantly, "they're out having tea on the lawn. Gad, won't Justinia be surprised." I dissembled my feelings and followed unresisting, for there is no avoiding fate.

II

This ignoring business gets a trifle fatiguing after a fortnight of it. If Justinia would be downright insulting, I could manage my part all right, but she's too cute to let people talk. Nobody has the slightest idea we are ignoring each other as hard as we can go, yet once apart from watchful eyes, she gives me to understand in that indescribable manner peculiar to her sex, that she meets me under protest.

Beastly underhanded I call it.

I was soliloquising thus one morning in the billiard-room, knocking the balls about viciously, when Randal found me.

"Why, what the dickens are you doing here, old chap? Rest started half an hour ago—thought you were with them."

"No," I said. "I'm not, what's to do?"

"Why, the whole party are off to Branton Woods—ruined castle, don't you know, pic-nic afterwards—wife's idea—come on."

"Thanks, my dear fellow, but I think I'll stop behind and have a quiet day."

"Nonsense," said Randal, as he buttoned on his gaiters, "come along with us."

"Fact," I answered, "I've a beast of a head on me."

"Oh, well," and he flourished his whip towards the brandy, "if you feel better later on, have the mare saddled and ride after us, don't forget." Saying which, he vanished.

"I'll be hanged," I exclaimed as his horse hoofs died away, "I'll be hanged if I stand her treatment any longer, I've a good mind to get back to town first thing tomorrow."

So saying, I pitched away my cigarette, and wandering into the library, sank dejectedly into a chair.

"I wonder," I soliloquised, as I filled and lighted my pipe, "what she can see in that ass Graham? The man's an arrant fool, and yet the way she looks at him sometimes, and gets him to fetch and carry for her—it's disgusting!"

I sighed, and, taking up a magazine, began to read. I had almost reached the climax of the story, when the door opened and someone entered softly.

At first I took no notice until, hearing the rustle of a dress I craned my head around a book-case, and beheld—Justinia.

I fairly gasped with surprise. She was turning over the magazines with her back to me; presently she selected one, and drawing up a chair, began to read.

Her face was still turned from me, but by leaning back I could see the outline of a round, soft cheek, and a pink little ear, half hidden in masses of chestnut hair. So I sat and watched her, puffing thoughtfully at my pipe.

Suddenly in leaning a trifle farther that I might catch a glimpse of her profile, the confounded chair creaked loudly. She started, turned, and saw, me. An angry flush crept into her cheeks, and for a moment I thought she was going to speak; but no, she turned away and became immediately interested in her reading, taking no more notice of me, than if I had been a piece of furniture.

This annoyed me, and noting how the smoke from my pipe drifted towards her, I puffed more fiercely than ever. It was after I had emitted a somewhat denser volume than usual, that I fancied I heard a little cough. Straightway I became possessed of a most unholy joy, and redoubled my exertions.

Ha! There could be no doubt of it this time, Justinia coughed distinctly and undeniably. I immediately became interested in an advertisement for a patent soap on the cover of my magazine. Her chair moved farther away from me with an angry little jerk. Heavens! I could have yelled in my triumph. Suddenly she rose and faced me indignantly.

"I hate a pipe," she said icily.

I looked up from the soap advertisement in simulated surprise.

"Yes," I assented, "most girls prefer cigarettes, I believe. Permit me," and I extended my case.

She stomped her foot angrily. "Will you put it out ?"

"My pipe? Certainly if it really inconveniences you—" But ere I could well finish she had swept majestically from the room, a tiny handkerchief held to her nostrils. My pipe was perhaps a trifle foul, but not so bad as that. Presently, seeing the soap advertisement had lost all attraction for me, I rose, took up my hat and sallied forth into the sunshine.

I wandered about for an hour or so, vaulting stiles and crossing meadows, until, feeling lunch would be acceptable, I turned back. The path led through a wood, which I guilelessly followed, until, having walked some distance, I stopped to look about me, and reluctantly confessed to myself that I was lost. I sat down, therefore, and lighting my pipe, waited philosophically for some honest yokel to come and direct me.

Five minutes had barely elapsed, when hearing the snapping of twigs, I turned and beheld—not the yokel I expected, but Justinia.

Instinctively, I got to my feet, and raising my hat, opened my mouth to speak, but her cold little nod forbade me, so once more I subsided upon my log and watched her out of sight.

"Now I wonder what brings her here of all places?" I said to myself; "hang this ignoring nonsense! She might have shown me the way back, and I'm awfully hungry, as it is, I must wait for the 'yokel' I suppose."

Half an hour elapsed, and I was knocking the ashes out of my second pipe, when again the bushes parted, and again Justinia appeared—this time from a totally opposite direction.

Her hair had come loose from its fastenings, and escaped from beneath her hat in a confusion of curls. I noticed also that her dress was torn by the brambles, and altogether she seemed tired and miserable.

That she was lost I was now certain, and I felt sorry for her despite her treatment of me, and determined to offer my assistance, I rose therefore inspired by this kindly thought, and took a step towards her. She turned at the noise and saw me. In an instant the tired look vanished, she made an involuntary movement to hid the rent in her dress, and without deigning me a second glance, walked on down the path.

For a moment I had some idea of following; then I sat down again—fuming.

"First thing tomorrow I go back to London," I vowed, "I'm sick and tired of the country, and then—" At this moment, I was interrupted by an approaching whistle, and the long-expected yokel appeared. He stopped at my question, and pulled a hand from his pocket to stroke his chin.

"Ay, zur," he said, eyeing me slowly all over, "there be two ways to 'Unston Grange, so there be. Go straight along that path till you be coom to the clearin', turn to yer roight, and t'will bring yer out by t'great dyke—but doan't 'ee go that way, zur."

"Not?" I enquired.

"No zur—it be difficult to cross it be—turn to yer left through Dean's 'Oller, 'cross the home meadder—"

"Thanks," I said, rising.

"Home meadder," he persisted, "cross t'bridge—"

I nodded and walked on down the path.

"Bridge," he shouted, "turn to yer roight and there you be." Herewith the whistling recommenced, growing fainter and fainter until it was lost in the stir of leaves, and the drowsy hum of insects.

'Half-past one,' I said, consulting my watch, "and she's been out ever since eleven, lost beyond a doubt, and wandering round in circles." I admit I smiled, it really seemed such poetic justice.

But my merriment was short-lived for, turning a bend in the path, I came upon a lonely little figure, seated on the stump of a tree. She was labouring at the shoe in her lap, and I saw a little silk-stockinged foot peeping out beneath her skirt.

Such an advantage was not to be lost, and I promptly stepped forward. A dry stick cracked beneath my tread—she looked up with a start and the foot disappeared like a flash as I stopped resolutely before her.

"Can I be of service?"

"Oh, no thank you," she answered carelessly. "That is," she continued as I turned away, "this wretched heel has come off." I sat down beside her at once, in a matter of fact, brotherly sort of way, and taking the little shoe, turned it over in my hand.

"Hair-pins, my dear girl," I said, glancing at the twisted remains of the one she held, "though a wonderful tool in the hands of a woman, are not of much use in an emergency of this kind." And I smiled indulgently.

"But what am I to do? I can't walk without a heel."

"Of course not," I agreed, "I shall have to knock off the other one also—permit me," and I leaned over to unfasten the other shoe. Justinia demurred strongly. I pointed out with unerring force and logic, that it was impossible to fix a heel with a hair-pin, and an ordinary pen-knife, whereat she presently yielded up the other shoe, and with heroic calmness watched me prize off its heel, which I furtively dropped into my pocket.

"Now," I said, "allow me to replace your shoes."

Justinia was all indignation in a moment.

"Very good," I said, slipping them into my pocket after the heels, "if you don't mind waiting an hour or two, I'll hunt around and have them properly mended, though I fancy you could walk in them, if you tried."

"I think you are horribly mean," she exclaimed angrily. I agreed that meanness was undoubtedly one of my chief characteristics, venturing at the same time to touch her ankle. Seeing it was not withdrawn, I slowly fitted on the shoes, and felt distinctly sorry when she rose.

"Excuse me," I began, "but I fancy that left one is not quite right; I've no wish to detain you, of course, but if you will just let me take it off again—" but she turned away indignantly and hurried down the path. I followed.

"D'you know," I said, after we had walked half a mile without exchanging a word, "do you know, I begin to think you are angry. Is anything worrying you?"

Justinia stopped to gather a spray of hawthorn blossom, maintaining a frigid silence.

I felt annoyed and distinctly uncomfortable.

"It's—er—it's wonderful the difference a pair of high heels makes," I said desperately.

"Indeed."

"Yes," I replied feebly, "you don't—er—even come up to my shoulder, do you?"

Justinia quickened her pace without replying, and a silence fell heavier than before.

"Justinia," I broke out at last, "don't you think this has gone on long enough? Haven't we ignored each other sufficiently?" She became extremely interested in the sprig of hawthorn, twisting it between her white fingers.

"So you didn't go to India after all?" she said, without looking up or noticing my question.

"Well, no, I didn't," I replied, apologetically.

'And why?"

"Well, you see, India is such a confounded distance away, and I thought if ever you did happen to change your mind—"

"I shall never do that," she broke in.

"Then of course there is no more to be said," I answered stiffly.

"Do you know, I think you are very ridiculous," she said, which remark I though entirely uncalled for. Thus it was in the deepest of deep silences that we at length reached the clearing. Remembering the 'honest yokel's' lucid directions, I turned unhesitatingly to the right.

Presently, sure enough, the dyke came into view, stretching away on either hand as far as the eye could reach; my triumph was complete. I felt sorry now that I had not 'tipped' the rustic handsomely.

Justinia came to a sudden stop, and gave an exclamation of surprised dismay.

"It's only the dyke," I said reassuringly.

"Yes, but how horribly wide; however am I to get across? Surely there must be another way round?"

"Certainly," I said cheerfully, "if you care to walk another—er—two or three miles."

Justinia looked at me in desperation.

"How am I to cross the hateful thing, it may be awfully deep."

"Yes, of course," I said, readily.

"Then what is to be done? I can't walk another mile in these shoes," she said dolefully.

"You might try swimming it," I suggested.

"Kindly talk reason, Mr Hartrick."

I bowed. "Jumping may suggest itself to you—"

Justinia turned away with a stamp of her foot.

'—though I should scarcely recommend it myself, "I pursued. "No, it seems to me that, swimming and jumping being altogether out of the question, there remains but one way."

"And that?" she enquired with a swift side glance.

"I shall have to carry you over, of course."

She declared that the idea was utterly preposterous.

"Oh, very well," I said, "then I must try to find another 'honest yokel' and get him to bring planks and things, I suppose. It may take a long time, but of course, since it is the only way, why, the sooner I begin the search, the better," and lifting my hat, I turned away. I had gone but a few steps, when a quiet little voice reached me.

"Mr Hartrick."

I walked on stolidly.

"Dick."

I turned back instantly. Justinia looked at me with a pair of beseeching eyes.

"Is there really no other way?" she asked humbly.

"Absolutely none."

"But you'll get frightfully wet," she said, retreating as I advanced.

"I'm afraid so," I sighed, "but I must put up with that."

"Do you think," she began, "do you think you will be able to—to—" here she stopped, blushing and stammering most delightfully.

"Well, that depends," I answered. "I carried you easily enough, you remember, that time you sprained your ankle, about a year ago, though I suppose you have grown lots heavier since then. Still, I'll do my best." So she suffered me to lift her.

The man is a born fool who could not turn such an occasion to good account; still, I determined to take no risks. Clasping her tightly to me, I stepped into the water, and making for a large, round stone in the middle, got upon it.

"Justinia," I said, "look at me."

She gave me a quick, shy glance beneath her long lashes.

"I am now," I continued, "standing upon a stone, Justinia—a smooth, round stone, and may slip off at any moment."

"Then get off it at once," she commanded.

"No!" I answered, "here I stand until either we fall off, or you promise to marry me."

Justinia hid her face, and perhaps it was as well she did so, for her red lips were provokingly near, and it required all my attention to keep my balance.

"I am waiting, Justinia."

"Then you must tell me first that you—you—love me," she said, her face still hidden.

"Good heavens!" I exclaimed, "you know very well I have been trying to teach you that fact for the past three years and more."

"But you never told me so."

"Never told you so!" I echoed.

"Never once," said Justinia, stealing a laughing glance at my perplexity.

"But I thought you hated all that kind of thing?"

"And forgot I was a woman."

"I often wanted to tell you—er—things, about—er—loving you and all that, but somehow I never dared, couldn't get them out, and, oh, what a preposterous ass! I've only kissed you once in all these years."

Justinia laughed. "Hush!" she said, "don't call yourself names, sir, and now, do please take me to the bank."

"First, let me tell you that I do love you, more than I can ever tell you, with all—"

But her lips were somehow nearer than ever, and—well, I found it easy enough to keep my balance after all.

"But Justinia," I said, as I reluctantly set her down, "supposing I had gone to India?"

She looked at me with a laugh dancing in her eyes.

"Ah—supposing," said Justinia.

THE BOOKS OF JEFFERY FARNOL

The Broad Highway
The Money Moon
The Amateur Gentleman
Chronicles of the Imp/My Lady Caprice
The Honourable Mr. Tawnish
Beltane The Smith
The Definite Object
Our Admirable Betty
Some War Impressions/Great Britain at War
The Geste of Duke Jocelyn
Black Bartlemy's Treasure
Martin Conisby's Vengeance
Peregrine's Progress
Sir John Dering
The Loring Mystery
The High Adventure
The Quest of Youth
Epics of The Fancy/Famous Prize Fights
Gyfford of Weare/Guyfford of Weare
The Shadow
Another Day
Over the Hills
The Jade of Destiny
Voices From the Dust
Charmian, Lady Vibart
The Way Beyond
Winds of Fortune/Winds of Chance
John o'the Green

A Pageant of Victory
A Book for Jane
The Crooked Furrow
The Lonely Road
The Happy Harvest
A New Book for Jane
A Matter of Business
Adam Penfeather, Buccaneer
Murder by Nail/Valley of Night
The King Liveth
The 'Piping Times'
Heritage Perilous
My Lord of Wrybourne/Most Sacred of All
The Fool Beloved
The Ninth Earl
The Glad Summer
Waif of the River
Justice by Midnight (completed by Phyllis Farnol)
plus innumerable short stories and articles.
Farnol also wrote the forewords to two promotional books: *Hove* and *Portrait of a Gentleman in Colours*.

About the Author

A brief introduction to the late Jeffery Farnol is given in the Foreword.
Jane Farnol Curtis is his daughter, now living in Australia, and the possessor of many of her father's original ms and other memorabilia.
Pat Bryan is the author of the definitive biography of Jeffery Farnol, Farnol: The Man Who Wrote Best-Sellers.

0-595-23421-6